Lock Down Publications and Ca$h
Presents

QUEEN OF NAPTOWN 2
ALL HAIL THE QUEEN

Written By
KEITH CHANDLER

First Edition 2025

Printed in the United States of America

This is a work of fiction. Names, characters, places, and incidents either are products of the author's imagination or are used fictitiously. Any similarity to actual events or locales or persons, living or dead, is entirely coincidental.

Lock Down Publications
P.O. Box 944
Stockbridge, GA 30281
www.lockdownpublications.com

Like our page on Facebook: Lock Down Publications
www.facebook.com/lockdownpublications.ldp

Stay Connected with Us!

Text **LOCKDOWN** to 22828 to stay up-to-date with new releases, sneak peaks, contests and more…

Like our page on Facebook:
Lock Down Publications

Join Lock Down Publications/The New Era Reading Group

Visit our website:
www.lockdownpublications.com

Follow us on Instagram:
Lock Down Publications

Email Us: We want to hear from you!

Dedications

I would like to dedicate this to my brother, Donnie. R.I.P. God, I wish you could give me twenty-four hours, so we could ride and laugh at all these cowards. We could hit the liquor store, park, and just talk for hours, then I could show you half the niggas you knew have died when they lost they power.

Them same niggas forgot about you, bro, after they gave you them flowers. I'm sitting here with a face full of tears. I never thought that pain lasts this many years. One thing I have learned from all this is niggas and family are fake.

I'll rep yo name til I die. Feel me? I sat back and watched how everything changed since you got killed.

Wish I could bring you back for one day. Take you around to show you the niggas that claimed they loved you just turned they back and walked away. You was too loyal to them niggas, and in the end, you got killed. Them same niggas owe you a lifetime, but still, they don't check on Mom, but then again, you wouldn't want them to check on her because they out there rocking with the same niggas that put you where you are. I lost all respect for them, but it's good. I love you, bro.

Chapter 1

Queen

Me, Tif, Porsche, and SK rode through the streets of Indianapolis, trying to come up with a plan. While us girls talked, SK was going through his bag of guns he had gotten from his house. For every gun SK had in the bag, he had a thirty-round clip for it. For the plan I was coming up with in my head, those thirty-round clips would be perfect.

After Duke's dad passed away, he moved out of the house they had and moved into another house in the hood on West 25th Street. Nothing had changed since Duke moved into his new house. It was still the hangout for anyone that wanted to party. We parked the car on 26th Street, and all of us got out, as SK put his 3DR Solo Quadcopter drone in the air. We watched on the screen SK held in his hand, as people partied on the block. They were having the time of their lives. No one paid attention to the drone, as it hovered over their heads, seeing everything that was going on. SK brought the drone back to us, and we took it back to the car and grabbed up our weapons, so we could join the party too.

"Tif, since you already in the driver seat, stay in the car and keep it running. If you see anybody come this way, let that thing go without question because we not sparing anything," I told Tif, as I shut the door.

SK, me, and Porsche stood behind a house that was being built on the block.

We could see Duke's whole house from the spot we were at.

"We need to block all these people in, so I think we should come from the top and bottom of the block, and I come heads on so that way if anybody try to run, they will get knocked."

"I don't have a problem with that. I'm going to take the top of the block," Porsche said, taking off up the block.

I kissed SK on the lips and took off down the block. Once I hit the block, all I heard was shots been fired. SK was running across the street, gun blasting at everyone.

Boom! Boom! Boom! Boom! Boom! Boom!

Without even thinking twice, people started trying to run up and down the block to get away, but that was hard to do with me and Porsche coming on the block. SK was already on the porch, waiting on us, by the time we hit the front of the house. As soon as we made it inside Duke's house, SK let two shots off, killing a female who was in a chair watching T.V.

Porsche hit Duke's cousin, Fresh, in the face as soon as he stepped from around the corner. SK took to the stairs, as me and Porsche crept our way toward the kitchen.

Boom! Boom! Boom!

Three shots rang past our heads, hitting the door frame.

Whoever it was doing the shooting was ducked behind a thin counter, thinking it was going to save them but not today.

Boom! Boom! Boom!

I let three shots go from my gun, making sure to hit the middle of the counter. The body of whoever was hiding hit the floor extra hard. We kept low to the ground, as we made our way into the kitchen, but as soon as we walked inside, we saw a door shut and noise coming from the room. I looked at Porsche, who gave me a head nod. We both already knew someone was behind that door, so we made our way toward it slowly. I stood on one side, while Porsche stood on the other. Porsche grabbed the doorknob and was about to push it open when shots began ringing.

Boom! Boom! Boom! Boom! Boom! Boom! Boom! Boom! Boom! Boom!

All ten shots hit things inside the kitchen.

As soon as the shots stopped, me and Porsche didn't waste any time letting our guns go off inside the room. We heard something hit the floor and knew we got whoever it was in there. When we opened the door, Duke's body sat on the floor with holes all over his body.

"Come on, sis. We gotta get out this bitch," Porsche said, as SK came running into the kitchen with his gun in the air.

"Let me handle this. Hold tight," SK said, turning on the gas stove and then lighting the curtains on fire on the way out the door. We could hear the police moving in close.

We ran back to the car where Tif was waiting with the car running. As soon as all our asses hit inside the car, Tif peeled off, toward Martin Luther King where police cars zoomed by.

"Where we headed to now?" asked Tif, as we continued to wait at the stop sign on 26th Street.

"The police is about to turn the heat up in the hood behind this, so while they are attending to the murders and fire, we need to continuing hitting these bitches. We can handle all the business right now," I said.

"Head towards 36th and Kenwood to one of my little cousin cribs so we can park my car and hop into something else. My daddy have many cars sitting in the back of my cousin's, so we going to get one of his," SK said.

When we pulled up to SK's family's house, we all hopped into a dark blue Lincoln truck that had tints. On our way to handle our next mission, we doubled back past Duke's house and saw the whole block taped off. Instead of turning down the block, we headed toward 26th and Highland and then turned left until we were on 28th and parked.

Money's brother had a weed crib that sat in the middle of the block, so we parked where we could see everything that was going on. He had a little traffic coming and going. When everybody was gone, we all hopped out, and Tif knocked on the door. He opened the door without even asking who it was, while he talked on the phone, and that cost him his life.

SK pushed Tif to the side and put two slugs into his face. I had taken the Queen out of a deck of cards. I soaked the card in Money's brother's blood and left it on top of his chest, so the streets would know I wasn't playing any games. I knew I was egging the police on like I was untouchable. I grabbed his phone on the way out of his house.

Money's mother stayed around the corner, so she was next on the to do list. One way or another, Money and them would have to pop out.

While I stood on the side of Money's mother's house, I texted her from her son's phone, and the text said, "I been shot. Come to the house but no police so hurry up, Momma."

Ten minutes passed before Money's mother came rushing out the house with Marilyn's sons.

"Here's the deal. We not going to kill the woman, but we are going to make sure she understand we not playing no games," I said to Porsche through the Bluetooth I had in my ear. Porsche stood beside the house. We continued to watch her put the kids in her car, and as soon as she shut the back door, I was on her back in seconds.

I put my gun to the back of her head.

"Ahhh!" screamed Money's mom.

"Shut all that fucking screaming out before I kill you out here and I'm not playing with you," I said, twisting her around, so she could see I wasn't playing.

"I don't have anything you would want but a few thousand dollars in my pocketbook," she said, crying, thinking this was a robbery.

"Bitch, do it look like I want some fucking money from you?" I asked.

"If that's not the case, then what is it that you want because I'm in a rush to get to my son? Please tell me why you have a gun pointed at my head," she asked.

"Call you son, Money, on the phone," I told her.

"I know who you are. You the woman that used to date him. He told me about you," she said with fear in her eyes. She put her purse on the trunk of her car and searched for her cell phone.

"Hello?" Money picked right up.

"Money and Marilyn," she said, crying harder.

"Mom, what's wrong with you? Are the kids okay? Why you crying?"

"I'm standing outside the house, and there's two ladies here with guns pointed at me. I was on my way over to your brother's, and they said they wanted to talk to you."

"What? Who has guns on you? Mom, what's going on?" asked Money.

I stood there, listening to Marilyn on the other end of the call, cussing and screaming out orders to whoever was there.

"Tell that bitch ass girlfriend of yours that she can stop sending rookie ass niggas to kill me and just come to handle it herself if she want it done," I said into the phone. Money's mom's hands were shaking bad.

"Who the fuck is this?" Money demanded to know.

"Stop playing bitch ass games with me because you know damn well who the fuck this is," I said.

"Queen?" he asked.

"You hit it on the money. This is Queen-Bee. So, ask your baby momma why we going to continue to play weak ass games. She send people to me, and I will keep sending them back to y'all in body bags. I have a lot of money so buying ain't even hurting me. You can keep hiding like a bitch, but me, I'm in my hood showing love," I said.

"Queen, I don't know nothing about what you and Marilyn has going on, just don't hurt my mom and kids. I don't understand why you have her at gunpoint," Money said with his voice shaking.

"Just put Marilyn on the phone," I said, tired of listening to Marilyn in the background.

"What, bitch?" she said into the phone.

"Don't forget I'm here with your mother-in-law and the kids so I think I have the upper hand right now. Listen and shut the fuck up. You sent people to my doorstep to kill me for nothing. You started this, so I'm going to finish it," I said.

"What you talking about don't mean shit," Marilyn said.

"You keep talking slick, this woman and kids will be meeting Big Jesus and Kim. Yeah, that was my work, and it felt good to see the fear in Big Jesus' eyes before I pulled that trigger. I'm trying to see you face-to-face so stop playing games," I said.

"Bitch, I'm where you want to be," Marilyn said.

"Meet me at our old house," I said, knowing she knew what I was talking about.

"I'm there." *Click.* Marilyn hung up.

I dropped Money's brother's phone onto the trunk. "I'm sorry they put you in the middle," I said, cutting through the back of the house.

We hopped in the car, and Tif peeled off toward our crib. When we walked inside the house, Sade had cleaned up the house. The house smelled like cleaning supplies.

"Where the bodies at?" I asked, shocked to see them gone from the floor.

"Girl, you know I got connections. They somewhere in White River. You be forgetting my brothers ran this city for years," Sade said.

"Well, thank you. I'm about to strap up and meet up with this bitch, Marilyn, so I can end this shit," I said.

"I hope you don't think you going to meet that girl by yourself because I know she's coming with her team." Sade followed me into the room.

"Yeah, bitch, that ho about to show up deep," Porsche said.

"I already know," I said.

"I got a plan. Let me set the pick on that ho. I already know how I can get her to come to us," Porsche said.

"How?" I asked.

"She's greedy, so I'm going to text her and explain how we beefing, and I'm thinking about robbing our stash spot. I'm going to let her know I'm trying to join forces with her, so we could get you out the way. Y'all know that ho is going to go for that," Porsche said.

"You think she will go for that at this moment, even after her mother-in-law said it was two females that had her at gunpoint?" I asked.

Chapter 2

Porsche

"Okay, bitch, I have this Thompson M-1 that's equipped with a one hundred fifty round drum that comes with it. I want you to take this with you into the house and just wait until I bring the bitch inside, plus we have to see if she bring a group of people with her, so she can do the triple cross on me," I said to Queen, as we passed a blunt back-and-forth on our way to a house on Goodlet. This was the same house I was going to tell Marilyn to meet me at, so we could rob Queen of her money and dope.

For the last thirty minutes, I had been texting back-and-forth with Marilyn, putting it on her thick. I knew Marilyn was geeked that I was texting her, trying to rejoin her team. Marilyn wasn't really a killer, but she knew I was, and with her back on the team, the sky was the limit. Marilyn couldn't wait to get on with the plan I was talking about.

"Marilyn just texted and said give her twenty minutes, and she will meet me while she send a grap to y'all old house to get you," I said to Queen, as we pulled in front of the house.

"It's nothing," Queen said, rushing out the car and into the house.

I shot to get something to eat while I waited on Marilyn to pull up. I ate her KFC while sitting in the parking lot. Since KFC was only five minutes from the house, I was going to stay there until Marilyn pulled up then make her wait for another few minutes before pulling up.

***

It was a little past 9:35 p.m. and pitch dark outside when I pulled back up to the house on Goodlet on the west side. I parked my car a few houses down. Before I stepped foot out of my car, I checked her twin .45s because she didn't know if Marilyn had men surrounding the house. Looking around, everything seemed good, so I stepped out the car and took steps toward the house, but before I could make it into the yard, I heard a horn. Turning around, I saw the headlights to a car flick a few houses down. I already knew it was Marilyn. Marilyn sat in the car by herself, smiling and waving her over. I acted like I didn't know who it was.

"It's me," I heard after the car window came down a little.

I walked over to Marilyn's Jaguar and jumped inside.

"Bitch, you look good as shit! I missed you so much, and I'm not going to lie. I was mad at you, but as I sat back and thought about things, I started to understand the way you were thinking. But at the same time, I felt like we been through a lot, and you turned your back on me when Queen came home from prison. We were thicker than anyone," Marilyn said, leaning over and hugging me tight.

"Yeah, when Queen laid out everything you and Big Jesus did to her, in the back of my mind, I was thinking what would you do to me when the time came if Queen is your blood? I do understand you will always choose yourself over anyone, which is what you supposed to do, but at the same time, I didn't understand how you would keep this from me for so long. All them late nights we set up on the block, getting money. But fuck all that shit, bitch. Queen been going all type of nuts on people. I let the bitch know that y'all both was wrong and shouldn't be gunning at each other the way y'all have been. Stuff have gotten out of hand and shouldn't have never made it to this point, and when you sent them dudes to get her and missed, she really started feeling herself.

I hollered at her one night about y'all having a sit down to clear the smoke in the air, and she snapped. She stopped talking to me, selling me bricks for a while, but then, we made up again, and that's when she told me she killed Kim and Big Jesus in they house that night. I didn't even know it was her that did that until we started drinking, so that was my breaking point. I let her know she was becoming a new person. The bitch put me out of her car and told me if I didn't like the new her then fuck me and don't call her no more, so I came up with a plan to just hit her where it hurts, and that's them pockets. I know she haven't moved that shit yet because it's too much," I said.

"After this shit, we going to be back with the bag. It's only the two of us anyway, so let's get this shit over with, and by the time we load everything up in the cars, Queen will be gone from us," Marilyn said, hopping out of the car.

I walked toward the back of the house with Marilyn on my heels. I grabbed the key I put under the flowerpot that sat on the doorstep and unlocked the door. I flicked the light on as soon as they walked inside the house.

"Follow me, sis, it's in one of the back rooms," I said, still leading Marilyn into the biggest trap of her life. I walked into one of the rooms that had a lot of boxes in it, and Marilyn stepped in line right behind me. When Marilyn crossed over the door frame, she was hit in the back of the head hard.

***

Queen

Marilyn hit the floor, holding her head. She kept blinking but couldn't stop her head from spinning or stop the black and white dots she saw every time she opened and closed her eyelids. She saw a figure standing over her. When she was able to see again, I was there, smiling down.

"Queen! Please. We're family, more like sisters. I know I have crossed the line, but we both have done shit to hurt one another. We can look past everything and just move forward. I'm sorry. Please don't kill me," Marilyn said, begging for her life.

I stood over her, laughing at how she could sit there and fix her lips to say she was sorry.

"Bitch, I almost got killed fucking with you, but now you sorry. Well, I'm sorry too. I'm sorry that you missed when you tried to kill me all them times," I said.

"We can link back up like old times and take over the whole Midwest. You have the best dope, and I have some connections, so we will be able to reach far. It would work best if we could work together. Just trust me again please," Marilyn cried.

"You a snake, so we will never be able to link back up. Your daddy was a snake too, so you must go link up with his bitch ass," I said, putting two shells in her head.

I stood there, just staring down at Marilyn, as blood dripped from the big hole.

***

Me, Porsche, Sade, and Tif sat on the sofa, smoking on some blunts, talking. We were all scrolling through the net, and a breaking news alert popped up.

"Today in Indianapolis, the police have been busy on the northwest side of town. First, there was a report that shots were fired inside a house on West 30th Street. When officers arrived at the house, they walked up to the front door wide open with a lady lying dead in a puddle of her own blood. Officers went to secure the house and found another body on the side of the house, who was a male victim. Officers believe the male victim was trying to get away by climbing down from the rooftop.

"Not even twenty minutes later, officers were called to a house on West 25th Street, a few blocks down, where a fire broke out, and bodies were lying in the streets from gunfire.

A witness told officers that three people came on the block and started shooting at everyone. Then, they ran into the house, and all anyone heard were gunshots. There were multiple shell castings found in an encampment area of the house. The bloody night of violence drained the police as another call came in that people were shooting at each other outside a house, authorities said. Reporting from Foxx 59 News."

"Damn, it's been a long day," I said, resting my feet on the coffee table.

"Hell yeah, and Sade, you should have seen how Marilyn IQ exploded out the side of her skull, speckling the wall with blood and gray matter," Porsche said, laughing.

While we talked, I texted SK to see if he was good. He responded that he was and that he loved me. That put a smile on my face.

"Bitch, what you smiling about?" Sade asked.

"Something SK said. That's all."

"Sis, SK put in that work today. He's a whole different type of nigga," Porsche said to Sade.

Chapter 3

Queen

Now that Marilyn and her team were out of the way and not being a problem for us anymore, it was time for us to get our heads back in the game and get back to the money. We were living life in the fast lane and stunting on everyone that wasn't part of the team. We didn't know where Money was hiding but hoped he didn't pop his head up and try his luck and end up like Marilyn did. We all knew that with him still around, he was going to be back. We had caused him and his family too much pain, but in the meantime, we weren't going to stress ourselves or put any time in trying to locate him.

***

We had been so busy handling business that the girls never had spare time to make it up to the dealership to trade in their cars. After they left for the night, I grabbed one of the trash bags and started counting. The trash bag came up to $315,000. When I was done, I hopped in the shower and climbed in bed with a smile on my face.

Around 11:30 the next morning, Sade pulled in front of the house to pick me up. We were meeting Porsche and Tif at the dealership around 1 p.m.

The dealer came walking out the building, as we were parking our cars.

"Hey, you just left here the other day! What you trying to do? Start your own dealership?" he said, smiling at us.

"Don't worry yourself about what I'm doing. Worry about how you going to count that money in that bag my sister has in her hand. We both know you like that money, so you know what I'm here for," I said.

"Yeah, we trying to hop in something sexy and new," Sade said. She tossed the duffle bag, and he peeked inside. A smile began to form on his face.

"What you trying to ride out in, Sade?" I asked to see what she had in mind.

"Really, I don't even know yet, but I need something that's silly. Whatever we all get, we have to come fresh because we have to stunt hard. Niggas be in Benz and shit, so I'm tired of that," Sade said.

"Man, we already been riding in these cars you have on the lot. You have anything else we can check out?" Porsche asked the dealer.

"Yes, we just had some new cars shipped in this past weekend. We haven't had the time to ride them from the back. I know for a fact not too many people are riding these. I only have five of them back here so follow me, so I can show y'all," the dealer said, walking toward the back of the building. He pushed the gate open after unlocking it, and my eyes locked in on a triple black Maserati Ghibli.

"Bitch, them are the new Maseratis. I was just looking at one of these on my phone last week. They on the market for about $70,000. I'm so in love right now," Porsche said, being the car freak she was.

I knew Sade already had one, but these niggas and bitches weren't riding in these, plus they just came out. By the time people in the city started riding these, it would be a year or two, and by that time, we would be in something else. When I used to be in the car with Sade on the highway, she would hit the gas, and the car would hit eighty-five miles per hour in a few seconds, and I loved that.

"I see that look in your eyes again. They nice," the dealer said, standing next to me, still holding the duffle bag tightly like we were planning to take the money back and say fuck the cars.

"Yeah, I'm in love with that all-black one. It fit me to a tee," I said, watching the girls check out the other cars.

Porsche was walking around an all-white one with red insides, Tif had her eyes set on a smokey gray one with the same color inside, Sade was sitting inside a dark blue one with white insides, and the last one we planned to grab up for SK. Copping the last one was really so no one could be riding them but our crew. Plus, he had been putting in work for us without thinking. We were all thankful for his help.

"Bitches, we about to be pulling up and shutting the city down with these new cars," Tif said, still walking around her car.

"We going to take all five of them. It's $315,000 in that duffle bag, so that should cover for the cars and the paperwork, so can you please hurry up and go draw our papers up, so we can hit the city?" I said, looking at the dealer.

"It's time to get our heads back on this money. We shut business down for way too long to get that business in check, but now that it's over, we have to hit the streets running," Sade said.

"That's the talk I like hearing. Let's get to the money," Porsche said, rubbing her hands together.

Sade had to go inside the dealership, so she could give the dealer her address, so he could get her and Porsche's cars towed to her house. Plus, she was grabbing our keys.

She came out and handed us our keys. We all started up our cars.

"We goin' to meet y'all back at the crib after we handle this business. Just make sure y'all have shit ready to go when we get there. I'm about to open the road up with this bitch," I said, smashing out the parking lot.

Me and Tif switched lanes and turned every head we rode past. We rode that road like we were the only ones out there the entire time we were headed to the airport. We knew damn well we shouldn't have been driving these cars the way we were, but it was impossible not to when you had two hundred on your dash. We slowed down as we neared the airport because airport police stayed ducked off in the cut sometimes. We pulled into the tarmac where Roast's plane was sitting in the back. Roast wasn't anywhere to be seen as we parked. He was always standing next to the plane, waiting on us, so we just sat there and waited. We were like ten minutes early anyway.

Not even a few minutes later, Roast came walking toward us with a few guys following behind him. As soon as Roast saw us waiting on him, he gave the guys a head nod, and they went right to work, unloading the airplane and putting the coolers inside our trunks and backseats. While they put the coolers in place and Tif talked to Roast, I took the time to go place the duffle bag under Roast's seat.

Tif and Roast talked for a few more minutes before they hugged and said their goodbyes. We hit the road on our way back to the hood, but this time, we made sure we did the speed limit the whole way back.

Chapter 4

Me and Tif pulled up on West 28th back-to-back, and I was so happy that we made it safely. That little thirty to forty minute ride always scared me to death, driving with all the dope.

When we pulled up, all the kids were around Porsche's and Sade's cars. That made me laugh because I remembered when that was me years ago. Every time we got a shipment in, we all made an agreement to give back to the kids in the hood, so we would grill food and give out drinks to those who needed the help. We also helped people with clothes, shoes, and bills. I learned from Black Jesus that if you showed the hood you cared, they would always show it back to you. We weren't going to be like the other crews out here and just take without giving back.

"Go help with them coolers." I heard Sade tell a group of boys that were talking to some young girls in front of the house. Without any back talk, they came right over and started grabbing shit from both cars. This shipment was a little different than all the rest we had had. We grabbed some other drugs so that we could corner the whole drug market in the city. We ended up copping ten bricks of uncut coke, ten uncut kilos of heroin, two bricks of Molly, five kilos of fentanyl, twenty pounds of kush, forty pounds of synthetic weed, and some liquid, synthetic weed, so we could spray it on paper to send to people in prisons that we dealt with. Every one of us was going to get a little of everything to hustle.

We all would put money up in the pot after every shipment and the rest we just split down the middle. Since we didn't have to pay someone else to cook for us, we were getting all the extras. I was a master at cooking or fixing the dope now. I was going to whip up all the dope and just double everything up so that way whoever bought the dope would be able to do whatever they wanted as far as stepping on it. I could put more on the dope, but the product our team had was a brand.

I had been in the kitchen for hours, mixing and cooking, when Sade came in.

"Damn, you in here making all type of noise," Sade said, as I was finishing up the last two bricks of coke we had.

"I know. I'm trying to hurry up and get done because I'm tired as well," I said, wiping sweat from my face, making sure not to touch it with my hands.

It was so hot inside that kitchen that I had stripped down to my panties and bra.

"Bitch, look at all this dope in here," Sade said, seeing all the paraphernalia that lined the kitchen counter and table.

"I'm glad I'm done with this shit," I said, as Porsche and Tif stepped into the kitchen as well.

"I see you in this bitch looking like a chef, sis," Porsche said, laughing at her own joke.

"Okay, this the deal, y'all. We all get two bricks of coke, two bricks of crack, and five kilos of heroin apiece, so that's going to leave us with two bricks of coke, two bricks of crack, ten kilos of heroin, four pounds of fentanyl put up in the safe. We also have three bricks of Molly, which y'all can figure out what to do with because I don't know anything about that shit. Now that spray, we just going to sell sheets of paper for $50 apiece," I said, nodding to the team. They started grabbing up all their dope since it was already together and stuffing it inside their duffle bags.

"I need you to take a ride with me real fast, Queen," Sade said, as we began cleaning up with bleach. We wiped down everything.

Once we were done, me and Sade grabbed up our shit and jumped in her Maserati, so we could make our rounds around the city. We had to shoot to the east side of the city. Sade's little brother, who was locked up in the federal prison, had a few connections out here that he wanted Sade to pull up on for him. He still had a lot of love and respect out on the streets and needed Sade to connect the dots for him. The streets were talking, and Sade's brother had the streets on lock. He thought his sister was just out there, working a job. He never knew she was grinding the way she was since she always kept a good job.

We had all types of people throughout the city grinding our dope, but this nigga we were about to meet had his hood on lock, so we were going to link up with him to see what he was talking about. He had only been home from prison for a few months and was getting to the bag.

Sade turned heads as she pulled down 10th Dear Barn to holler at the nigga, Bob. She parked, and we hopped out and walked to the front door. There was some young, bad, white chick sitting on the porch, smoking. Just as Sade was about to knock on the door, a female came brushing past us.

"Like I told you before, you don't have shit going for yourself to get a sample of this good dick. And when you do get something, you know where to find me at," Bob said, laughing and taunting the female, as he stepped on the porch. "Oh, shit. What's up, ladies?" asked Bob.

"We ain't on shit. I told my brother I would pull up on you when I get my shit back in order so here I am now," Sade said.

"I'm glad y'all pulled up because I'm down to my last and was about to go cop me something from my dude. Really, I didn't think you would pull up. I thought you were just talking since it been over a week."

"Nah, I don't talk just to be talking. I'm more of a action girl. But I love money too much. You in the streets, so you hear our names ringing. Anyway, what your pockets looking like these days?" Sade asked, getting right to the point of her being there.

"I need me at least a brick or more because my spot be rocking," he said.

"So, your mans been serving you! What he been charging you for the bricks?" Sade asked.

"Sometimes, he will be on bullshit and hit me for thirty but on a good day, twenty-eight. The dope is so-so."

"Well, look. This is my sister, and we talked on our way here. Since my brother gave us the okay and his word on you, we will charge you twenty-five for a brick of crack, or you can pay thirty-six for a brick of coke. Here's a gram each for you to try or have your people test it. We already know what it's hitting on."

Bob yelled for the white chick to come inside, and when she did, he handed her the gram of crack. She went right to work, setting up her things. She put the whole gram in her pipe and hit it hard. At the same time, Bob snorted the coke and leaned his head back with a big smile on his face. The white girl's whole face was twisted to the side.

"That's that butta right there. Hold on. I'll be back in a hot second," Bob said, rushing toward the back of the house. When he returned, he held a bag and handed it to Sade.

"That's $98,000, so I need two coke and one crack. I also need some of that good ass weed y'all got."

I went out to the car to grab his dope, so we could get out of there because we had been in his spot longer than needed. After dropping his dope on the table, we were out the door and into the car.

"All these niggas about to be copping from us. The way I see it, we should open some spots throughout the city to pump the weed. The dope we can continue to sell whole since we already getting the dope so cheap. Let these other people feed they families," I said.

"After we flip this shipment, we all should sit at the round table and add up all this bread and go big. We have connections outside of the city between us. We can get us a few bitches that work in these clubs and have them pushing shit through there too," Sade said.

"I need you to pull on Brookside, so I can holler at my nigga. Lil' Ricky's name been ringing hard throughout the city. Then, after this, I need to pull on 49th Street."

"What's good, Queen?" Lil Ricky said, coming out the house with a gym bag in his hand. For the bag in his hand, I gave him another bag that contained two kilos of heroin, ten pounds of loud, two cokes, and two cracks.

"I ain't on too much, trying to get big time like you," I said, smiling.

"Stop it. Everyone knows Queen got all the streets, honey," Lil Rick yelled, walking off.

"Bro, hold off. You know anyone that deal wit' the Molly because we got a few of those things too," I said.

"Yeah, hand me one of those joints. I got a few people that gets down," Lil Ricky said.

"Cool, just drop me the $30,000 for it whenever you ready for me."

We rode all the way to Keystone then down 38th Street, so I could go meet up with my nigga, Davo. He had just come home from prison. His case got overturned. He was a player and got to the money, so anytime he got something from me, I always showed him love. He only dealt in heroin and the weed. He would grab up two to three bricks of heroin, each for $55,000, and pounds of weed for $750 because he got more than twenty at a time.

In just a few hours, we dumped work through the whole city. Porsche was out south, doing her networking, while Tif took her networking out north. Her mother's side of the family were all in the streets, so she would be good. We, as a team, did good for the day.

Chapter 5

After we handled the problem we were having with Marilyn, me and SK had a big fight about him wanting me to move into another house, and I wasn't trying to hear any of that shit.

SK didn't feel safe inside the house since dudes had been in there, trying to kill us twice. I knew he was speaking the truth, but at the time, we were at war, but that was over. Then, he went on to say that I was a sitting duck by staying inside the house and getting the type of money I was getting now.

Sade picked me up, and we rode toward SK's job because I hadn't talked to him. He wasn't texting me back or picking up my calls. I knew he was reading the texts because I could see from my phone that he opened them up.

We pulled into the parking lot, and I jumped out. I made sure my clothes were on point before walking inside.

"May I help you?" the lady at the front desk asked, as I stood in front of her wearing a million-dollar smile.

"Yes, you know the person that drives that Maserati?" I asked, pointing to the parking lot.

"Girl, don't even waste your time. All the ladies in this building been trying to get they nails inside him, but he just keep it pushing. He would smile, and that's it. We heard he had a girlfriend, but he don't ever bring her around, but I will go get him, so you could try your luck," she said, walking toward the back.

I was standing there, killing them with my outfit. When me and the girls went to Saks and Neimans to get some clothes, I got me a few different outfits. I was dressed in a Polo shirt, Polo pants by Brioni, Christian Louboutin heels, Cartier watch, Cartier frames, handbag by Michael Kors collection, and a splash of Flower Bomb. I even had Sade lay my hair out for me.

It had been a whole month since the last time I talked to or had seen SK. I knew he was mad at me. For that month, all I did was grind hard to keep from thinking about him. We upped our game and had seventy-five percent of the city getting their dope from the home team! We were dealing with these cats my cousin connected us to from G.I. named Boy-Boy, Man-Man, and Lil Nut. They all were folks. Together, they ran through the underworld of G.I. like the wind. Lil' Nut was the wild boy that stayed high off the wets. Boy-Boy was the think on it for a hot second but end up fucking something up just because he could type. Then, Man-Man was the better one, but he stayed fresh. He was the laidback one. He always kept a group of bitches with him.

We even connected some dots with my cousins and had the prison system on lock. We sprayed them sheets and sent them inside, and they went like hot cakes. Dudes were buying thousands at a time. They said it was the best that hit the system that far. Life was good for us all.

SK came from around the corner, looking finer than all outdoors. His face showed that he was shocked to see me standing there.

"What's up, Queen? It been a whole month." he said, not giving me a hug or a kiss. I tried my luck and went in to give him a hug, but he stepped back.

"What's wrong with you?" I asked.

"I don't know what type of niggas you dealt with in the past, but I'm not the one you can just say fuck then show up weeks later to my job like shit is all sweet, trying to hug and kiss me. No female have ever treated me that way, and I'm not going to start letting any now. I'm a good dude that loves hard," SK said with an attitude.

"Baby, I know you're a good dude. That's why I'm standing here about to beg you to forgive me. I'm really sorry for the way I treated you. I miss you so much and love you to death. I just want things to go back to the way they were. Please, baby?" I said, flicking my eyes at him.

He pulled me into his chest and kissed me. When he pulled back, we heard clapping, and when we both looked up, the lobby was filled with females watching us.

"They like you, I see," I told SK.

"That was a good scene right there," the lady at the front desk said.

"Shut up, Candace," SK said, smiling.

"I'll be right back," SK said, kissing me before going to the back.

"Girl, you have a good man there. Any of us would love to have him, but you got him hooked," she said.

"You ready to go?" SK asked, walking with his gym bag in hand.

"Yeah, I had Sade drop me off," I answered.

He opened the passenger side door for me. He must have just washed his car because it smelled good and looked shiny. At the red light, he grabbed me and kissed me passionately on the lips. We held hands, while he drove. We were on the north side of town, cruising past some nice-looking houses. Looking at the houses pass, at that moment, I felt I could move out this way. There wasn't a lot of loud music, gun shots, or people awake all hours of the night.

"I want to show you something," he said, turning into a driveway of this big house then parking. We got out, and I followed him up the stairs to the front door, which he unlocked with a key on his chain. I looked at him sideways, and all he did was laugh at me. Once we stepped inside the house, the first thing I noticed was a big, oversized picture of me as I stood there, speechless.

"Welcome to your castle," he said, handing me a key.

"What?" was all I could get out of my mouth.

"It's okay. I would be speechless too if I were you. I got this crib after the first time you got shot at. I knew from then on we were going to be together. I also knew it was going to be extra hard for you to move out of your dad's house. That house been in your life since you were little, so I understand, but that was why I never said anything about this crib. See, before I went off to prison, my name was ringing bells in these streets. I know these streets, so I knew, at some point, you were going to have to move anyway, and when you saw it that way, I had us. I knew you didn't want to listen, just like the rest of you young bucks out there," SK said.

I stood there, crying my little eyes out.

"Why are you crying, baby?" SK asked me.

"I'm so happy to be your woman. You treat me the way a queen is supposed to get treated. You always seem to touch my heart, and when you said you already knew we were goin to be together, it's pulled my heart in a good way," I said, wiping my face off.

He walked over to me and hugged me tight. "I love you. Go check upstairs and I will be up there in a little while," he said, slapping me on the ass.

When SK walked into the room, I was sitting in the middle of the bed, rubbing on my clit, moaning his name. He was out of his clothes in seconds and standing at the foot of the bed, stroking his dick. I took my fingers out of my pussy and sucked the juice right off. He climbed into the bed. I moved out of the way, so he could lay back, so I could control what was going to happen. I took his dick into my mouth and went to work sucking the skin off of it. I knew he was about to nut after a few minutes of deep throating him. He was pumping inside my mouth like he was fucking a pussy, but I didn't want him to nut just yet, so I let go of his dick. Grabbing me and scooting me on top of his face, he started sucking my clit. I rocked my hips back-and-forth like I was dancing to a song. After a few minutes of him sucking my pussy and me stroking my clit, I was shaking and cumming all over his face. I hopped off his face and positioned myself, so he could fuck me from the back. I spread my ass, as he slowly entered inside my wet pussy.

"Shit, your pussy is so tight and wet," he said, sliding his whole dick inside of me. "Fuck," he sighed as he slowly stroked my pussy harder, sending his balls to hit my pussy.

"Fuck this pussy and stop playing with it," I pleaded.

He started hitting me with fast and hard strokes, hitting the bottom of my pussy. He now had both of my ass cheeks in his hands. While he stroked my pussy, I played with my clit, rubbing it hard. I looked over my shoulders and saw that SK had his eyes shut closed.

"Open them eyes and look at all this ass bounce on that dick," I said, throwing it back extra hard on him.

His eyes popped right open. He stared into my eyes for a hot second. I bit down on my lip, as I felt the nut coming.

"Fuck... me... harder..." I moaned, cumming all over SK's dick, turning it white.

I felt his dick begin to jump, so I knew he was about to nut, and a few strokes later, I felt the cum shoot deep inside my pussy. We laid in the bed, sweating and out of breath.

"I love you, baby," I said.

"I love you back," SK said, wrapping his arms around me.

Chapter 6

Me and SK sat down and had a long talk, so I had to make him understand where I was coming from on not parting ways with my dad's house. That was the only thing me and Kenya had left of his things, plus the house had been in the family for years. I did see the points he was making about me not staying in the same house, so I talked with Porsche about her little cousin renting out the house. Her cousin had two young kids and was looking for a place to stay, so I said yes to her moving into the house.

SK had work to do out of town at this club. His security job had been jumping for him too. He felt that since me and the girls had been grinding nonstop without a break that it would be good for our minds, bodies, and souls to take the trip also, so we could get a little rest. Me and the girls talked about it and decided it was a good idea to take a few days' break.

Being in Chicago for the few days was going to give us time to be free from the streets, and we would be able to do some more networking in the new city. Everybody knew them Chicago niggas knew how to get some money, and with the dope I had my hands on, I knew we could make a lot of money together if we linked up.

We were trying to show Chicago how we people in Indianapolis stunted hard, so we all drove our own cars. When those Maseratis pulled up in the parking lot back-to-back, it seemed like the whole world stopped in place, as we hopped out. You saw half-dressed females getting their holla on, while the niggas did their thing also, parking lot pimping. Since SK was security at the front door of House Of Blues, we were let right into the building without any problems.

While on the highway, I had texted Mookie and let him know I was hitting his city and where I was going to be that night. He told me to check the V.I.P. section when I got into the club.

There were people all over the club when we walked in. Everybody was having a good time with drinks in their hands. The diamonds started dancing as soon as we stepped foot on the dance floor. The lights flicked with the diamonds, and the club turned to see who we were since our style screamed "important". I looked up toward the V.I.P. section and spotted Mookie chilling with his guys and some bitches, so we made our way up toward his section to let him know we were in the building. Plus, I needed to put a bug in his ear about some business while the girls chilled back.

"What it do, sweetheart? I seen you and your girls step in looking like new money," Mookie said, meeting us at the top of the stairs.

"I'm good, just trying to get this bag and make sure all my peoples get rich in the meantime," I said, leaning in to give Mookie a hug.

"I been hearing your name coming up in many circles, and I must say your name been screaming loud and clear. If Black Jesus were here today, he would be happy you are standing on your own ten toes and that his bloodline still have the underworld in a lock," Mookie said, sipping on his drink.

"Really, I wouldn't be doing this if he was here with us today. I picked this hustling up because I wasn't going to sit around broke, and I knew my mom was too fucked up behind my dad, so I just played the cards that was on the table for me," I said, meaning every word.

"How is your mom doing these days? I haven't seen or heard from her in so long. She stopped by the house one day in some big ass clothes, and I gave her some money, but I didn't see her again."

"I know you heard she was off drugs, so with me doing the shit I'm doing, I needed her out the way, so I moved her out of town with my family. That way, she could get clean, and I can get this money. But I need to holler at you on some money stuff since it's enough to be made for us all," I said.

"Go head, let me know what's on your mind," he said.

"You said it yourself that you been hearing my name ring bells, so I know it could only be good. Since your ears are always to the streets, you know I have the best dope on this side of the map. I'm getting my dope at a good price, but me and the girls been trying to spread our wings and expand our business into your city because with all the dope I'm getting my hands on, there's not enough dudes in my city that can buy it all wholesale. I'm hollering at you because I didn't want to just step on your toes, so bottom line is if you could help me connect some dots while I'm down here, and we all eat," I said.

"I hear what you're saying, and I can help you and your girls out, but it all depends on the price you going to tax us for the dope, and the grade has to be better than what the city is getting now. If everything is good, we could do some big business. As you know, I don't be in the streets like that, but my partner, Lo-Lo, will be the one that gets at you," he said.

"The dope is so good you can step on it at least two to three times, and it will still be grade A. I only be stepping on the bricks once, and the city is eating it up. I have a kilo of heroin for you to try or give to your guys, and when you done, just get at me. I know you going to love it," I said, smiling.

"I got you then and will grab that before I cut out. So, in the meantime, enjoy yourself and have fun," Mookie said, going back to his guys.

I went to grab the girls up, and we hit the dance floor to blow some stress off. Every dude in the building was trying to dance with us, but we laughed and continued to party with each other. We were having a nice time. I saw Mookie give me a head nod twenty minutes later. The club was due to close, so me and the girls headed out before the rush. I kissed SK and let him know I loved him. I met Mookie at his car to give him the kilo, then we headed to our Airbnb we rented for the weekend.

Two days later...

We had so much fun in Chicago this weekend, but it was time to get back to the city and get back to that money. Mookie called me and placed an order, saying he hadn't seen dope that good in years, and that put a smile on my face.

Before we could step foot out of the Airbnb we had, Sade got a phone call from Bob, telling her that the homicide detectives were posting videos and pictures of us all on the news and social media. Once she got off the phone, she gave us all the details of what was going on in the city. We all hopped on our phones to see what social media was saying.

"Why the hell they looking for us?" Tif asked.

"They only looking for Queen and Porsche. They posting the stuff because that's all they have of the girls. They saying they found Marilyn's body inside a house," Sade said, reading her phone.

"Damn," I said, looking Porsche in the eyes.

"If they found Marilyn's body and they looking for us, then the nigga, Money, or his mother is talking to the police because they the only ones that knew we were meeting her, and when she didn't show back up, that's when they knew it was over with. You should have let me get at that nigga years ago," Porsche said with fire in her eyes.

"It's all fair game now when we hit the city," I said, grabbing up my bags by the door and heading to my car.

Chapter 7

Since SK wasn't staying at our Airbnb, I had to call him and let him know the news we had just received, and he flipped the lid. He told me to continue to rent out the Airbnb for a while. That way, it would give him time to get back to the city and see what was going on, but as he talked and we listened, we all were shaking our heads no. None of us were okay with just staying in Chicago and doing nothing. Us girls talked it out and decided that we would go back home but stay ducked off and only move when we had to.

Even with the police only looking for me and Porsche, everyone in the city knew Sade and Tif were part of the BBGM crew, so the police wouldn't think twice about fucking them up in the process, just to get their hands on us two. It was time for us all to put up our cars and get something lowkey to move around in since we were the only ones riding Maseratis.

While riding on the highway back to Indianapolis, me and the girls stayed on Zoom, talking and laughing. We all hit the city limit back-to-back.

"Okay, ladies, let me get off this Zoom, so I can call my mom to check on her. I love y'all, and if y'all need anything, just hit my line, also if something comes up. Don't forget we ducking off," I said before saying my goodbyes and hanging up.

I dialed Kenya's number and waited for her to pick up.

"Hello?" She picked up.

"Hey, Momma. How you doing down there?" I asked her.

"I'm doing good, baby. Right now, I'm chilling with Punkin, smoking me some good weed."

"Momma, I'm calling to let you know that the police is looking for me and Porsche."

"Queen, what do y'all girls have going on in that damn city?" Kenya asked.

"A lot been going on in the city that it's crazy. Really, it's too much to explain, so long story short, Big Jesus and Marilyn is dead. Marilyn baby daddy told police it was us who killed Marilyn. I don't want you to worry yourself, but I came back to the city after dropping you in Miami and turned the heat up in the streets. I starting taking over a lot of hoods in the city. Marilyn and Big Jesus were the ones behind me going to jail because Big Jesus was fucking the officers on my case. They been plotting against me the whole time, and plus, the letter I got from Dad explained a lot to me, so I took care of what he was talking about in it. I just wanted to hear your voice and to let you know I'm good. I love you," I said.

"Baby girl, I know you going to be good, but why don't y'all come down here, and we figure it out together? As a mother, I'm worried about you every day. I'm getting myself together, so I can be up there with you again. I know I fucked up before, and I'm sorry for that. I was weak at the time, but that was then, and this is now. There's some things I need to talk to you about that I did while on dope, but when we do sit down, promise me that you will have an open mind when I lay everything on the table. Anyway, where are Marilyn's kids at?" she asked.

"Like I said, Money probably has them since he's working with the police. But let me get off this phone, Momma. I love you and will see you soon," I said, hanging up the phone.

Sade and Porsche were the only people that knew where our house was, so I wasn't all that worried about the police coming to that address. I wasn't even going to let Tif know I moved out the old house because SK expressed his feeling on how he didn't trust Tif, but Sade and Porsche were his sisters. I sat a block down from the house, just watching everything, making sure stuff was good.

I pulled into the driveway and quickly ran up the stairs. The first thing I saw when I rushed inside was SK sitting in his La-Z-Boy, eating some chips and watching the news. They were talking about us showing out at the Christmas party. They posted pictures and were showing small video clips of us showing money, drinking, and having a good time. All these clips came from other people posting us. The headline read: BBGM Are Known to the City as Queen Pins and They're Wanted for a String of Homicides and Selling Drugs. I was glad they didn't say anything about having any witnesses.

"So, you saw what they are saying?" SK asked, looking up at me.

"Yeah, I heard them, but how could they be on us when we covered our steps?" I asked.

"I don't know who they got their info from, but you'll need to figure this shit out before it gets too hot," he said.

"I know, right?"

"Honesty, baby, I don't want to see you or my sisters in prison," SK said, walking up to me.

I looked up into SK's eyes and got lost for a few seconds.

"Baby, I'm never going back to prison again. I promise we will do all we can to keep from taking that trip," I said.

"Y'all just let me know if y'all need a hand or need something!

***

For the past few days, I had been inside the house, trying to put together what happened. I hadn't even stepped foot on the porch. We had been going through Bob to move the dope we had, and he was moving fast. Sade even paid her cousin to drop the dope off and pick up money when we needed.

I counted out 1.2 million and shot it to Sade, just in case anything happened. Then, I put another 1.2 million up for Kenya. I knew she would do what was right.

Word on the streets was that after Money got the news about his brother and Duke, he went right to the police. He learned that more people were dead when he walked into the police station.

"Damn, Porsche, I fucked up this time. If I would have let you get at that nigga years ago, we wouldn't be in the middle of this shit, but it's done now. Do anyone know where the nigga or his mom is staying at?" I asked.

"I put $100,000 on they head, so it shouldn't take too long for someone to get at us. I know everybody and their mothers are out there looking," Porsche said.

"That's coo. Just let me know what's up. I'ma hit you back in a little while when I get my mind right. Stay low and out the way, sis. You should try some yoga," I said.

"Yoga! Yeah, okay. I love you," she said, hanging up in my ear.

With Money and his mother helping the police build a case on us, if they snatched us up first, we were a done deal, so we had to move fast and get them first. The only problem we were having was that they could be anywhere in the city. There were too many places where they could hide the family. We would be looking for them forever. For all we knew, the police could have them in New York somewhere, chilling.

Chapter 8

Every channel I flicked to was talking about us like we were the worst thing the world had seen. I set the remote down and picked up my phone.

Scrolling through social media, it was the same thing. They had put a reward out for any information that would help them locate us that led to an arrest. It seemed like all everybody was doing was talking about us. When I saw them talking about that reward, I knew I wasn't taking my ass outside for anything. Porsche and them, on the other hand, wanted to continue to handle business in the streets like it was nothing.

If it wasn't for the help of Sade, I didn't know what I would have done. Sade had copped her a three-bedroom house two blocks away from us. Me and her talked, and I told her how SK felt about Tif, and she agreed with him, saying she only dealt with Tif because of me, and plus her dad was the man. She said Tif was a scared bitch and would crack under pressure.

While scrolling on my phone, it started ringing.

"Hello?" I picked up.

"Sis, I'm about to have this hoe, Tif, pick me up and take me to Sunset to pick up this bag," Porsche said.

"I don't think that's a good idea. You can't have someone else pick that shit up?" I asked, not liking it.

"Right now, everybody out doing them, so I have to move," she said.

"Well, if that's the case, you need to be safe and hit my line as soon as you walk your ass out that building. You know everybody knows who you are so make this shit fast, bitch," I said.

"Nobody going to know who I am because I have on my stripper outfit, and you know when I wear that, people don't be knowing me," she said.

***

Porsche

"Why the fuck you still riding around in this fucking car? You tripping hard, bitch," I said to Tif, as she walked down the stairs to the car.

"Bitch, I'm not the one the police is looking for, so there's no reason for my ass to switch up cars again. Plus, I'm grown, so I do as I please," she answered, pulling off down the street.

"I hear you talking, but when they snatch your ass up because of this hot ass car, don't be crying," I said, texting on my phone.

At that moment, Tif had me so hot that I wanted to pull my gun out and shoot her in the face for being so silly.

"I'm going inside this building only for a few minutes and coming right back out. I don't need anyone to see me so just keep the car running because I'm rushing out," I said, stepping out the car and walking into Sunset strip club.

***

Tif

"This hoe is tripping, thinking I'm about to just sit in this car, waiting on her," I said to herself, getting out of the car but leaving the keys inside.

I didn't like girls but thought they were sexy. Sometimes, I played with them but loved some dick. Girls were just fun for the time being.

"How you ladies doing? Mind if I sit here at y'all table? Drinks are on me," I said, waving a stack of bills in the air.

"Shid, have a seat. We ain't tripping," one of the ladies said, moving over to make room for me to sit. I waved three strippers over to the table and started making it rain.

***

The waitress at the bar saw it raining money and looked to see who it was, and when she saw Tif from the news clips, her heart started pumping, and her hands started sweating. She grabbed her cell phone off the bar and ran to the back where the music was on low. She dialed a number she'd locked in her mind.

"Are you telling me that one of them is there, inside the club?"

"Yes! She's making it rain at a table full of females. She's the only one that has three strippers as soon as you walk through the door. I'm the waitress at the bar," the waitress said into the phone.

"Okay, thank you. We're sending someone to check the club out. If you can, keep her there until a car shows up."

The waitress didn't care that she was getting someone locked up. All that kept running through her mind was that money they had been offering. She had already spent the money in her head. She went back to the bar like nothing had happened.

"I seen you on Facebook. You part of them BBGM chicks. They looking for your friends," one of the strippers said, making her ass clap in front of Tif's face.

Tif was so busy throwing money and having fun that she never saw the officers step inside the club. The waitress gave the police a head nod toward Tif's table. The officers rushed over to the table, pushed the strippers away, and snatched Tif to her feet.

"What hat fuck y'all doing?" Tif asked as the officers took her down to the ground. They put the cuffs on her extra tight.

"Stand this mufucka up," ordered one of the officers.

***

Porsche

I locked eyes with Tif after coming out of the back of the club. I peeped the whole play, so I reached for my twin .45s and began blasting. I didn't care if anyone saw me because I looked like one of the strippers.

Boom! Boom! Boom!

I hit one of the officers in the back. The gunshots caused the club to go into a panic. Everybody started rushing toward the exits, so I blended in with the crowd and made it outside.

"We have a officer down. The suspect has yellow hair," the officer said over his radio before running out of Sunset in pursuit of me.

"You, stop!" the officer yelled.

Boom! Boom! Boom! Boom!

I let off four more shots, hitting the mark as soon as he came out the door.

Boom! Boom! Boom!

Another officer returned fire.

I didn't know there were that many officers there. I ducked low, as I made it to Tif's car, opened the back door, and grabbed the AK-47 off the floor. It had a one hundred round drum on it.

"Let's party!" I yelled, popping up in the air, waving the AK back-and-forth through the parking lot.

Laake... Laake... Laake...

I hit everything in front of the gun. I knew I only had a few minutes to get away, so I hopped inside the Maserati and peeled out the parking lot. I sped up 16th Street, going toward what was called The Land. If I made it to the hood, I was good. The only thing I saw when I crossed over the bridge was red, blue, and white lights.

"Damn, you stupid ass bitch. I told you to stay in the fucking car," I said, sucking Tif out I she did sixty-five miles per hour down the street. I hit the side streets, just to be safe.

Chapter 9

Queen

I was standing in the kitchen, helping SK cook dinner for us. We were having tender steak and a warm farro grain salad with pomegranate almond with Mediterranean spice blend, Za'atar toasted sesame seeds, dried oregano, and thyme, along with tart Mediterranean spice sumac and a bottle of Soder Torn Sprite wine.

My phone started lighting up and sounding off, letting me know I had a missed text. I picked up the phone off the counter, and it started lighting up again.

"Hello?" I answered the phone.

"We have a big ass problem on our hands. Scroll through the internet but it was a shootout at the strip club tonight."

"What the hell you talking about, girl?" I asked, not remembering that Porsche had Tif take her up there to pick up something.

"At Sunset strip club, it was a shootout tonight," Sade said.

"I thought that girl was only going in to handle her business and get back out to the car. Where are them bitches now?" I asked, mad at myself for not stopping them from going.

"Porsche is here, chilling, rolling up a blunt, and Tif got knocked in there, partying."

"Sis, I need you to pull down here, so we can talk this shit out," I said, pressing end. "Baby, that was Sade calling to let me know that it was a shootout at Sunset. I already knew some bullshit was going to happen. That's why I tried to get Porsche to let someone else go pick up the bag, but she acted like she needed the money now," I said to SK, while we both scrolled through our phones.

Social media was going crazy on this story. They were calling Porsche the crazy woman. The shootout even made it to CNN news. I stood there, shaking my head, thinking about all the bullshit the police were stacking on us.

Me and SK were just setting the table to eat when the news popped up on the T.V.

"Breaking News, police say they need your help because they're in desperate need at this moment and will do just about anything to apprehend this group of ladies that go by the name BBGM Crew. Tonight, a few of our officers were taken down by an AK-47 that one of the ladies was shooting. These ladies are the reason our murder rate has gone up over the last few weeks. Right now, it's a tragedy that our officers were doing their job, and four bystanders are listed in serious condition. If you know anything, please call 317-212-TIPS. When we receive more information on this case, we will bring it to you first. I'm Jenny Smith reporting back to you in the station."

SK cut the T.V. off, and we began to eat our meal. I shook my head because the city was getting too hot, and with them continuing to pile stuff on top of our case, it would be hard to beat later down the line.

***

I watched Sade pull into my driveway off of my phone. By the time I made it down the stairs, they were walking through the door, and I started firing question after question.

"Damn, sis, I thought this was a in and out thing," I said.

Without even waiting on a response, I began walking back toward my office, and right away, I went to the bar to make us a few shots of Patron while Sade rolled up a blunt because shit was getting crazy.

"When I got inside her car, the first thing I did was cuss her out for not trading cars. Then, when we pulled in front of the strip club, I told the bitch to sit tight, and I would be back in a few seconds. When I walked from the back of the club, the police had Tif in cuffs in the middle of the dance floor. So, knowing the game, I shot my way out that building and now here I am," Porsche said.

"This shit is too much. It's so hot, and all we doing is making shit worse than what it is. We the only thing they talking about on the news and the internet. The police is going to end up shutting the whole city down until they get they hands on us. They not playing behind theirs getting killed. Then, this silly ass bitch got herself locked up, and no telling what they going to do to her when they get her in that cell," I said.

"She probably downtown, getting fucked up by the police. We all know they going to try everything in the book to get her to talk, so I'm glad she don't know where my new house is because no telling what she going to say for her freedom," Sade said.

"After getting off the phone with y'all, I had SK contact this good lawyer for her, so he should be down there as we talking now. She would be good for a while until we figure something out. I let her mother and daddy know what was going on. I let them know I was working hard on getting her home. I ended up transferring some money into her mother account, so she could take care of whatever," I said.

"The best thing to do right now is to get you two bitches out the city. We can hit the highway and duck off until this shit die down. They not looking for me, so I can continue to hold down the business until we figure out what steps to take next," Sade said, passing the blunt.

"I can't go anywhere. I need to be here to handle this mess because if I don't, then we just going to be fucked, but I do need you to drive Porsche out the city for me. I talked to Mookie before y'all pulled up, and he said you can come to Chicago where he has some nice houses ducked off, so you can go out there and chill for a while until this problem is fixed," I said, looking at Porsche.

"I'm not trying to be down there by myself, plus Mookie is your peoples, not mines, so I'm good on that plan. We on to the next plan please," Porsche said.

"To make sure you good, I will come with you down there. That way, you not by yourself, but I will only be there for a few weeks because I still have to work, plus I have two sons that I know I can't leave with my BD too long. So, let me call to tell him what's going on and to pack me a bag," Sade said, grabbing her phone.

"So, you just going to stay in the city, even after talking me to death about how hot we are and the police shutting down the city? I feel like you should come along too until that heat die down, and we all can come back to figure it out together," Porsche said.

"This shit has gotten deeper than just Money and his mother. We have the police blood on our hands now. I will be good. I promise that so just go down there," I said to her.

I went into the next room where I had a safe behind the wall and started counting out $400,000 and stuffed it inside the duffle bag with a pound of weed. Everybody had their own money, but the safe I just opened was all of ours. I walked back into the room and dropped the bag at the door. I texted them Mookie's numbers and told them to call him once they got to Chicago. When we hugged, it felt like it was going to be a long time until I got another one.

"I will see y'all soon. I love y'all," I said, sending them off.

Chapter 10

Detective Hernandez

Tif sat on the fourth floor inside an interrogation room in Indianapolis Police Headquarters downtown. She was seated behind a table in a steel chair facing the two-way mirror that the detectives stood behind, just staring. The detectives had the room so cold that Tif was shaking like a fiend that needed a hit.

"So, this is one of those girls that's down with that BBGM crew everybody want to be part of? They say this chick spend more money in one day on clothes and shoes at the mall than we make a year. Sometimes, I think we working for the wrong side of the game," I said.

I stood beside my partner, looking at Tif's diamonds flicker as she cleaned her nails. Detective Deer and I had been working day and night on this case since the first time Queen got shot around Christmas time. I wanted Queen bad. We wanted to get Black Jesus but he was too smooth for us, so with his daughter taking over, we hated her too. We were going to get her and her crew off the streets one way or another. We both knew if we were the first to put handcuffs on those girls that it would put our career in a new light. As we both stood there, the door burst open and in walked a nice-looking lady.

"Who are you?" Detective Deer asked.

"Hello, fellas, how are things today? I'm Amber Salt, and I'm here on the behalf of the F.B.I. director. We've been called, so we're here to check shit out," she said with a pretty smile.

"To check what out because this is our case, and we will handle everything ourselves? We don't need you F.B.I. people coming and fucking shit up for us," I said with a little bass in his voice.

"Us fucking shit up? Not! We're here to clean up all the shit y'all have stepped in. My boss was called for the help, so I'm here to talk to y'all suspect," Amber said.

"Hell naw, that's not happening on my watch," I said.

"It is happening on your watch, and I will show you better than I can tell you," Amber said, walking out the room and entering the interrogation room.

When Amber entered the room, Tif sat up in her chair. Amber walked circles around Tif, as she waited for someone to shut off the camera.

"You little bitch!" yelled Amber, grabbing Tif by the throat and choking her. Tif fell out of her chair and onto the floor. Tif's head began to spin.

Detective Deer and I stood, shocked at the way Amber was in that room handling business.

Tif's eyes started rolling in the back of her head, and Detective Deer started to get worried that Amber might kill her. She let go of Tif's neck and stood up.

"Get your bitch ass back on that steel," Amber said.

While she got up off the floor, all Tif could do was cough and hold her neck, as she sat back in her chair.

"You part of them BBGM bitches, so I know you know how to get at Queen. You hear me talking to you, bitch?" Amber said, backhanding Tif across the face, busting her lip.

Tif just laughed.

"You think shit is funny. You better tell me something now, or I promise you it's going to get ugly," Amber said, all in her face.

Tif looked Amber in the eyes with a smirk on her face and said, "If you keep putting your hands on me like that, you will see how ugly it can get out there."

Amber balled up her fist and started beating Tif's face in, drawing blood.

"You piece of shit, you going to give me Queen!" yelled Amber, while she continued to beat on Tif.

Tif's eye was swollen shut, her lip was busted, and she had big knots on her head. Amber didn't care about Tif, so she knocked her to the ground again and began to stomp her.

"Ahh, fuck! Bitch, stop!" screamed Tif in agony.

"Understand you in our hands now and until you give us information on your crew, shit is going to get worse for you. No one can save you from us, you little bitch," Amber said.

"You up on me, bitch, but you can't break something that don't bend," Tif said, laughing.

Amber bent down next to Tif's head and put her lips to her ears and said, "With you, I'm going to get Queen. She killed my man, Big Jesus, and I promise if it's the last thing I do, I will get her. We tried to send her to prison for the rest of her life, but that didn't work, and now, she still at the same bullshit, so you can help or go down with her. This is deeper than you think," Amber said, kissing Tif's ear, sending chills through her body.

Tif knew all of what Amber talked about because Queen told them everything. That kiss felt like the kiss of death. Amber stood over Tif, laughing. She pulled her gun out and pointed it at Tif's head.

"I could shoot you right now and cover it all up, so I suggest you start talking," said Amber.

"Get that gun out of my client's face and lay one more finger on her and I promise to have your job by the time the sun comes up," Mr. Louis said, stepping into the interrogation room.

Amber reluctantly pulled her gun away from Tif's face. Tif didn't know who the man was or who sent him, but she was glad he walked into the interrogation room when he did because a moment more and she would have been a dead bitch. As Tif was getting off the floor, Amber rushed past her, leaving out of the room.

***

Tif

"Hello, I'm Mr. Louis, and I was hired by your sister and parents. Sorry for walking in late. My last appointment took longer than I thought it would. But I'm here now," Mr. Louis said.

"Hello," I spoke back through a busted lip.

"Are you okay?" he asked me.

"Yes! A little fucked up. My ribs feel like they broken, but beside this, I'm good," I said, cracking a weak smile.

"I need someone to go get my client some ice now," Mr. Louis yelled, and a few minutes later, a detective came in with a cup filled with ice.

"Thanks," I said, sipping the little water that was inside the cup.

"I'm going to do everything in my power to get you out of this place. I know they treating you like shit. I'm not going to promise you anything. I told your sister the same thing I'm telling you. With some police getting killed, they can keep you locked up until they feel you had nothing to do with it," Mr. Louis said.

All I could do was put my head down and pray that I got to go home soon.

"You might have to sit for a few weeks until your sister handles her end."

Chapter 11

Queen

Me and SK talked as I steered my car through the streets. I let him know the plan I had on how I was going to gain the information to get at Money, and he thought it was a good idea. We pulled up a block down from Money's sister's candy store on Paris. We sat behind dark tints but watched her movement through the front glass window. Since the sister knew who I was, the plan was for SK to go inside and check the store out.

***

SK

I got out the car, walked up the block, and entered the store. There wasn't a soul inside the store at the time I went inside. Money's sister was wiping down the countertop when I walked up.

"Can I help you, sir?" she asked me, smiling.

"Yeah! Can you please grab me a big bag of Flamin' Hots, a bag of sour patches, two watermelon Crushes, and a pack of Now & Laters," I said.

Twisting around, she went to grab the things I asked her for, but when she turned back around to lie the food on the counter, her eyes popped out of her head.

***

Queen

I stood there beside SK with a smirk. She never heard or saw me come into the store and lock the door behind me.

"Queen! I don't have anything to do with that bullshit my brother and Marilyn are into. All I want to do is run my store, take care of my little ones, and keep everybody business out of my life," she said, looking at me.

"Money let Marilyn put you and the rest of y'all family in between the trouble they caused. Myka, I always liked you, but I need you to get your phone out and call to see where they staying at. I already know it's your mother, Money, and his kids. I need to talk to Money face-to-face, and I can't with the police around," I said.

"I already tried to get Money to tell me where they were staying at, but he wouldn't tell me anything," Myka said.

"Well, you need to try your luck with him again, or you need to talk your mother into telling you because your life depends on this information," I said.

"When he pick up, don't let him know we here and you better make sure you get a address before hanging up," SK said, eating some chips.

Myka grabbed her cell phone off a stand and called her mother. She put the call on speaker, so we could hear the call. She talked with her mother for ten minutes before she went into her spiel.

"Momma, I need to know where y'all at," Myka asked.

"Myka, I'm not supposed to tell you any of that," her mother said.

"Mom, really! I'm your daughter, and we all really miss you. How long you going to go with them people telling you that you can't see me or your grandkids? It's bullshit you will keep something like this from me," Myka said, fake crying.

"Whatever this shit is your brother has going on with the police, they have us staying here on lockdown, and they supposed to give Money some type of money. They told us after them girls are locked up, we could come back home and go on with our life. Them girls are really killers. They killed Marilyn, her dad, Duke, Duke's brother, and your brother too," she said, crying.

"I understand all that, Momma, but that's not important to me. You are! It could take the police forever to get their hands on them chicks. Plus, all that's going on, none of it have anything to do with you, so we might not see you for months," Myka said.

"You right. Okay, but you can't give this information to anyone because it could get us all in trouble. Don't even let your baby daddy know I told you this, but we been staying low out in Greenwood. The house is nice too. I'm texting you the address now as we talking. The only thing I don't like is the police sit in front and back of the house," the mother said.

"I just got your text, and I promise not to say anything to anyone," Myka said.

"How have my grandbabies been doing? Tell them I said hello and love them."

"I will let them know. They been asking about you and the boys. I told them you went out of town and will be back soon."

"Have you and their father been okay because we both know how he gets sometimes," the mother said.

"He been getting better. We good, Momma, but I have to go. Some people just walked into the store. I love you and will see you soon," Myka said, hanging up before hearing what her mother said. "I done everything that was asked of me, so can y'all leave me and my family alone? I don't care what y'all want this address for, but my deed is done. Here's the address," Myka said, writing the address on a piece of paper.

"Thank you for your helping hand," SK said, pulling his 9mm from behind his back and shooting Myka in the face. Her body laid behind the counter in a puddle of blood.

SK grabbed his snacks off the counter, and we rushed out of the building to the car down the block.

"I'ma hit a few guys that's looking to get their hands dirty for a small price. The only problem we have is that the police are in the front and the back, and we don't even know how many it is there," SK said, as I pulled off down the street.

"We have to figure this shit out like right now. Let them know it's extra in it if they can move tonight," I said, lying my head on the headrest.

SK was on the phone, networking, and doing his magic for me. He was talking numbers. My love grew deeper, sitting there listening to him go all out for me. I was really in my feelings because I didn't have my girls by my side. I knew if they were here, we would get the job done. I knew I could trust them.

I sat behind the dark tints and watched how the city continued to move around us.

We cruised up Martin Luther King, and I watched a police park on the street, and my heart started pounding. We turned down 28th Street, cruising really slow up the block, until we stopped in front of the house.

I grabbed SK's hat off his head, as I got out the car. I pulled the hat low over my eyes, as I walked up to my house. Porsche's cousin didn't answer when I knocked on the front door. I walked to the back of the house, grabbed the spare key we kept over the door, and let myself in. The house looked really good. I inspected the whole house to make sure nobody was there. I grabbed a trash bag and went into Big Jesus' old office, which was a kid's room. This was where the safe was. Even though the Lay-z-Boy boy was gone, I still knew how to open the safe that sat behind the wall. Once I moved the picture, I hit a button on my phone, and the wall opened up, revealing all types of guns.

I began filling up the bag with AK-47s, AR-15s, 9s, and extra clips. I made sure the wall was shut before grabbing another bag and opening the safe we had in the floor under the bed. I filled the bag up with money and did the same thing I had just done with the wall. I took both bags, set them by the back door, locked up the house, then carried the bags to the car.

As soon as my door shut, SK said, "Baby, the men will be ready in a few hours. They coming from Anderson now." He sounded like he was scared of something.

"Baby, please make sure you tell them we have to be on point. We can't fuck up shit because this move can cost us big time. No room for mistakes so I hope these dudes know how to handle business," I said, hoping I didn't have to kill one of them.

Chapter 12

Queen

I kept looking at my phone every few seconds, waiting on the time to meet up with the guys. When my phone hit 9:30 p.m., it was time to roll out.

"Baby, it's time for us to hit the road and meet your people," I told SK.

While we were getting in the car, SK got a text from his guys, letting us know they would be at the meeting spot in ten minutes.

SK and I talked the whole time we rode to the meeting spot. I was telling him the last of my plans when we pulled up to the warehouse on the east side of town. When we pulled in the parking lot, we saw two cars and several dudes standing around in all black. We got out the car, and SK began talking to one of the dudes.

"Aye, y'all, this is my lady, and she's the reason y'all are here. She really needs y'all help on some important shit, and I know this is the type of work y'all do, so this is the deal," SK said, enlightening the group of men on what our plan was that we had just finished talking about on the way here.

"So, y'all telling us that the police have the witnesses inside this house and that the police has the front and back on lock. If the police has the house surrounded, then how do y'all 'pose we get in there to get him and his peoples?" one of the dudes asked. He shook his head then started laughing like we had just told a joke, but we didn't see anything funny.

"Don't sit here and disrespect my lady again by sitting here, laughing in her face, because she is so for real about everything I just said to y'all. Her life depends on this move goin' good. So what if the police is around the house? That's why you getting paid the big bucks to handle it just like y'all do in the hood. I'm asking y'all if y'all ready to get y'all hands dirty, or did y'all waste our time?" SK asked.

"It's my bad for the laughing, but we always down to get our hands dirty for that cash," the leader of the group said.

"Good then! Here's two duffle bags. One bag has guns, and the other one has $250,000 in cash and a Pizza Hut outfit. One of y'all has to wear this outfit because this the way y'all will be able to get inside the house. Y'all have to steal a car for him to ride up in," SK said.

"One more thing! I want to see the job go down, so I need one of y'all to wear this phone around y'all neck. It's on FaceTime, and it's a burnout," I said, handing the phone to the leader.

They all piled inside their cars and followed behind us all the way to the address in Greenwood. We sat a block down from the house and watched the group park a few houses down. The phone was around someone's neck, so we could see that they were locking and loading their guns.

"I don't know how this shit going to play out, but let's get this shit over with," one of the guys said.

"Look, we about to go up in this bitch on some World War 3 shit and get it cracking because that's what we do. We get the job done," the leader said, holding the phone up to his face, but it was too dark inside the car to see him.

"Okay, this the plan. We goin' to spin around the block, drop one of you guys off, so you can steal a car and use it to pull back up like you have a pizza. While you in the front doing that, I need two guys to get the police in the back. Use as little noise as possible. After the back secured, then we work the front," the leader said, laying the plan out to them.

We sat and watched as a car pulled up in front of the house and parked. A dude jumped out, carrying a pizza box in his hand. He walked on the porch and saw two officers sitting in chairs, talking.

"Sir, no one called for a pizza from this address tonight," one of the officers said, getting up from his chair and walking in front of the door.

"Well, this the address I have on the paper, and if I don't delivery it, I will lose my job. I really need this job with my wife having our third child," the dude said with one hand still holding the pizza and the other hand inside his pocket.

When the officer looked at his partner, the dude shot through his pocket, hitting him in the stomach then aiming at the other officer before he could act on what had just happened. The gun had a silencer on it, so it didn't make any noise. When they were both down, he dropped the pizza box and went through their pockets for the keys to the door.

Me and SK sat down the block, shaking our heads at what we were seeing from the phone. Those niggas weren't playing any games. They were handling business. All the men ended up on the porch together.

Opening the front door with his gun in the air, the first dude stepped inside.

Boom! Boom! Boom!

He came flying right back out the door onto the porch. Another went right inside, spraying his FN from side to side, hitting an officer in the chest. The leader and another dude laid on their stomachs and crawled their way inside without getting hit. Cops were coming from everywhere in the house. Luckily for the first dude, he was wearing a vest.

Boom! Boom! Boom! Boom!

One of the dudes let off four shots in the direction of a cop that was ducking low behind the door frame.

While the others were busy getting at the police, the leader took to the stairs. He checked all of the rooms but one. When he pushed the door open, all he saw was the window wide open, so he walked over to it and peeked outside, but nobody was around.

"Damn, they got away," he spoke to us and took to the stairs. He had his gun in the air, as he took the steps one at a time. All the shooting had stopped, so he was making sure not to get laid out. He made it halfway down and saw his men and the police all over the floor.

"Freeze, drop the gun, and put your hands in the air," an officer said.

"I'm sorry but going to jail wasn't in my plans for the night," the leader said, letting his FN bark, but it just wasn't enough, as the officer was faster on the draw.

Boom! Boom! Boom! Boom!

The four shots hit the leader in the chest and neck.

Laaka! Laaka! Laaka! Laaka!

The leader's gun fired, as he went down to the ground.

We sat in the car, watching everything play out like we were watching a movie. I rolled the window down and threw the burner phone out, as SK pulled off, shaking his head.

"Fuck! Fuck! Fuck! Next time, they will not be so lucky. I need them dead," I said.

"We will get them, baby. I promise you that," SK said.

"I hope so because I need this shit to be over with like today. I'm so stressed out that it's driving me crazy."

Chapter 13

I was up all night long, just thinking about how Money, his kids, and mother all got away out the window. They must have already had a plan together because there was no way they were supposed to get away from the team of killers we sent up in the house. The family was blessed by God because it was going to get real ugly for them. The night was a waste of our time and money. SK felt bad for the team of killers because they put their lives on the line for us.

IMPD knew how much the BBGM crew wanted Money and his family's heads, but the disaster that happened last night only let the police know that our reach was longer than they thought it was.

I paced the basement floor, scrolling through social media, reading comments and thinking of ways I could get my hands on the nigga, Money. We had already killed most of his family, so he knew we weren't playing any games with him.

I read what the news was saying about us, and most of it was true, but we weren't as bad as they were putting it. We did our good deeds in the hood. They were making us out to be monsters. One news comment that I read said, "The BBGM crew are like the female Nino Brown without the snitching. If we don't work together, it will get worse. We have to confront this problem because if not, then the murders and drugs will continue to happen throughout our city. They been taking over the streets of Indianapolis, and from what we know, they are controlling eighty-five percent of the drugs coming into the city."

I stood there, just shaking my head. I didn't know where they were getting their information.

"Baby, it's a lady at our front door, asking if she could speak with you. She knew your name and also said something about she's your big cousin," SK said, showing me who he was talking about through our Ring bell.

Cousin Punkin stood on my doorstep in a business suit with diamonds flicking from the sunlight. She looked like old money.

"Let her in and show her the way down here for me please, baby. Thank you," I said, refocusing back to my phone.

"Hey, lil cousin," cousin Punkin said, strolling into the basement and twisting one of her dreds like she owned the house. She always put a smile on my face.

"Hey, big cousin. How are you doing?" I asked, giving her a tight hug.

"The question is how you doing? Every police in the city are looking for you and your crew," she said.

"Yeah, I know. That's why I have my ass inside this house. And cousin, how do you know where we stay at because, as far as I know, everybody still think I'm staying at the old house on 28th Street?" I said.

"Lil cousin, lil cousin, you should know by now that I'ma boss everywhere I go, and it's not hard for me to find who I'm looking for. I even know about the house your buddy got down the street. But I didn't know you girls were down here doing so good for y'all self. If your mother could see you now, she would be so happy. She doesn't know I made this trip because I knew she would want to stay. I'm here on business, so don't tell her you saw me," she said.

"I got you. You want a drink?" I asked, walking toward the bar to make a few shots for us.

"Give me something strong."

I poured two shots for her and two for myself, but she walked over and drank all four shots back-to-back, so I had to refill my shot glasses.

"My connect phoned me and told me that the city called in all the help they can get, so they can lock y'all asses up. They have the ATF, FBI, DEA, and the SWAT team will be on the ground soon," she said.

"Why are they calling them different police?" I asked her, not knowing how big the trouble we were in was.

"You and your team has y'all hands full with all these people getting killed. Then, it doesn't help that a few of theirs got knocked off. Plus, last night, some dudes ran up in the house where they were keeping that dude and his family at. I guess one of the dudes that was there kept saying that the family was dead, no matter what they did," Cousin Punkin told me.

"Okay, all the police are coming into the city, so what does that mean?" I asked.

"It could mean a lot of different things. They could lock the city down if they want to. It would be enough manpower for them to do that. When they do that, they put checkpoints throughout the city. People around the city already know who y'all are, so if they continue to post y'all, it will be hard for y'all to move. Lil cousin, y'all fucked up bad, but I know you will handle all that's coming," she told me.

"Damn, and they already locked up my girl, Tiffany, the other night," I said.

"Yeah, I heard about her, and my connection said she's coo for right now. I made sure that she gave Tiffany some food and let her know it came from you, and you got her."

"Thank you. I got her a lawyer that's good, but he told me it's nothing he's able to do for her right now," I said.

"The only way for her to get home is if you handle that snitch or turn yourself in, and whatever you come up with, y'all need to start moving fast."

"It's going to be so hard to get at them now. I don't even know where to start looking and best believe wherever they at, they have them guarded," I said.

Cousin Punkin lit up a blunt, and as soon as she hit it and let the smoke out, I knew it was some of that good Miami weed. It smelled so good that I got happy for a minute.

"Lil cousin, success at anything will always come down to focus and effort, and we control both of them. You can't let the other side win, but I guess the winner is the one who believes in the victory more, so you have to be fearless and don't complain, even when shit doesn't happen the way you like for it to. Just keep your head up and stay pushing. You have to find dude's weakness, and that shouldn't be hard to do," she said, passing me the blunt.

"All I know is that his brother, sister, a few cousins, and friends all got killed behind him, and now, the only family he has are the kids and his mother. When we pulled up on his mother the other day, I did see a pill bottle in her purse when she was searching for her cell phone. We made her call the nigga, so we could talk to him. The pill bottle had a Dr. Ross sticker on it," I said.

"See, then you go right there. You can get at the mother through Dr. Ross or his kids. Just give me a few days to about a week, and I will see what my connect can come up with for me. In the meantime, you better put up as much money as you can for all y'all because y'all goin' to need it if y'all think it's a slight chance y'all will walk away from this. Somebody going to do a little time," she said.

Chapter 14

The basement was where I went to do a lot of my thinking. After cousin Punkin left, I sat down there, thinking about all she said to me. She was a real boss bitch, and I had a lot of respect for her. She even took the time out of her day to come all the way to Indianapolis from Miami, just to check on me and lace my shoes up with some game. She was also helping me out by extending her hand to her connections. I picked up my burner phone and made a call.

"Talk to me."

"It's Queen. I need a shipment like yesterday," I said to Roast.

"It's a hard time right now. Plane down unless you can get down here and you still have to get it back yourself," Roast said.

"If I have to come there and get it back, that means the prices goes down?" I asked.

"Yeah."

"Okay then," I said.

"Well, my guy has his own plane and works for me, so he will fly through here in the next few days. I will set everything up for you and text you where you need to be," he said.

***

SK, Roast, and myself zoomed across the ocean water at top speed, hitting each wave in the speedboat we were on.

SK had a big smile on his face, as he looked up at the sun that was beaming down on us. He looked over at me and blew me a kiss, which I returned.

SK was treating the boat like it was an ordinary boat. The boat cost more than a house. This was about to be the biggest shipment we had ordered. I just hated that I didn't talk with the girls first. We were a team and always voted on things, but the streets were talking loud, and you couldn't mention drugs or money in the underworld if BBGM names weren't involved. I planned to step on everything in this shipment two to three times, so we could stack as much money as we could.

"Stop over there by that cone," Roast said, pointing.

SK stopped the boat, cut if off, and threw the anchor overboard.

"The package should be here very soon," Roast said, looking down at his watch and seeing that we were there a few minutes ahead of time. As he looked up at the sky, the airplane came across it. Roast watched black taped packages fall and land in the water, making big splashes a few feet away from the boat, making it rock.

Watching the packages hit the water, a smile immediately formed on my face. My hand started itching because I knew how much money we were about to see. Me and SK looked at each other again, already knowing it was time to turn up the heat in the streets.

"Grab that net over there," Roast said. I picked up the net and handed it over, so he could get the packages in.

"Anytime I can't come to you, you will need to remember this location because this is where the drop will be. Y'all the only two that need to know this," he said to us.

We helped him load the packages into the boat. Just as we were finishing up, another speedboat came across the water, approaching us at top speed. I looked at Roast then SK, who began to sweat. The Coast Guard pulled up next to us.

"Roast," one said.

"James," Roast said back to him.

Roast grabbed the black duffle bag off the floor and threw it to the Coast Guard.

"Is it all here?" the one named James asked, looking at the bag.

"Don't disrespect me again in your life," Roast said, starting up the boat and zooming off.

"We have to pay them every time we have to meet out here?" I asked, still watching the Coast Guard speed in the other direction.

"Hell yeah, if you want things to go smooth. With this flip, y'all should be able to walk away from the game rich," Roast said.

"Yeah, I know. I have to put some money towards your daughter problems, so she can get home soon," I said.

"Queen, since I met you, I grow to have love for you. You good with me. You not turning your back on your team just because the heat is turned up, and that, in my book, shows me what type of person you are. I been keeping my ear to what's been going on in Indianapolis, so I know you doing all you can do, so that's why I'm only asking you to pay me the $100,000 back. I just paid the Coast Guard an extra $150,000. This shipment is all y'all for whatever you have plans for," Roast said.

I couldn't do anything but smile and give Roast a hug. We were pulling up to the docks a few minutes later. SK kept trying to talk me into going to see my mother while we were there, but I felt it wasn't the right time. I began helping load the packages in the vans, and we rode off. Before we'd left the city, me and SK hired four old women from the hood to drive up to Miami and drive the dope back in the vans. Two vans held the dope, and the other two were just there. All four of the ladies jumped at making $30,000 a piece. That was probably the most money any one of them had ever had in their life. Paying $370,000 for this move wasn't anything. We were about to see millions when it all added up.

After SK made sure the packages were good, he sent the ladies on the way.

"Y'all drive slow, and we will be right behind y'all. We will make a few stops along the way," I said.

"Keep y'all phones on too," SK yelled.

"Come on, baby. Let's hit this road and follow these old bitches," I said, laughing.

"It shocked me how fast they said yes to this trip," he said.

"Them old hoes probably ain't never been outside of Indianapolis, let alone make $30,000 at once. They about to spend that money on bingo and beers as soon as we get back," I said.

Chapter 15

We turned down the block our stash house was on, and I let out a deep sigh of relief. Wiping the little sweet that fumed on my forehead, I unfastened my seat belt as SK pulled behind the vans the old ladies drove in. We made it all the way to the city without a single problem.

SK's cousins, Tyler and Penny, were already at the house when we pulled up. They helped us carry the packages inside the house through the back door. I paid the old ladies the rest of their money and sent them on their way.

"This the deal. I need y'all to get the fuck out my way, so I can get to work," I said, waving them out the kitchen while putting on my mask and gloves.

"Damn, baby, you going to put me out the kitchen too?" SK asked.

"Hell yeah, get the fuck out! I don't let anyone in the kitchen while I'm cooking. I love you but not going to show you the magic my mother showed me," I said, meaning every word.

At any time, SK could be gone and be with the next bitch, but the game Kenya gave me with this cooking would always be a part of me, no matter what.

"Okay, I love you and will be in the next room with these clown ass niggas," SK said, rushing into the other room.

I went under the kitchen sink and began to grab all the tools I was going to need to cook this shipment. I had to grab the mixing bowl, which I set on the counter, then had to grab out what I was going to cut the dope with from the cabinet, and then, I had to grab the B-12 and baking soda.

I walked to the table and grabbed one of the packages and bust it open by cutting down the middle with a knife. I pulled fifteen bricks out, placing them inside the mixer, making sure not to spill any. I weighed out 2,500 grams of B-12, tossed it inside the mixer, then added a little baking soda. I started the mixer and let it run on low, so it could mix really good, for a few minutes.

While the work was in the mixer, I poured some water into the cooking pot and grabbed four pyrex bowls. I weighed out nine ounces for each bowl. I put the magic touch on it, and the work turned into butter yellow crack with air holes in it. I did this same thing until all the dope was gone out of the bowl. I had turned the fifteen bricks into thirty crack bricks.

I was tired as hell from whipping all that dope but still had more to be cooked. After whipping the last few bricks, I walked everything over to the table and began weighing out the bricks and placing them inside Ziploc bags. I was dripping with sweat by now from weighing up the dope. I was going to step on the dope two to three times but decided to stick with how I had been cooking or mixing it up. After I was done with the crack, I had to move on to mixing the heroin kilos.

"Damn, bay, are you done in here yet?" SK asked, walking into the kitchen.

"No! Not yet. I still have a little mixing to do. I will be done in another half hour or so," I said, wiping the sweat off my face.

"You need to take a break and sit down because you been in here for hours, working hard," he said, grabbing a cold water and handing it to me.

"Thanks, baby! But why stop now when I'm almost done with everything?" I said, sipping on the water.

"Well, holler when you're done because them niggas have a few orders they trying to fill. The whole time we been in there, their phones been ringing nonstop," he said, going back into the other room.

My phone started to beep, so I went to see who was calling or texting. When I looked, I saw that it was Sade's little cousin calling, and I already knew what he was calling about, but he was going to have to wait for a few more hours, so I could get all this dope together. It took me about another twenty minutes, and I was done and ready to get the hell out of there. I lined up the work against the wall in order, so we knew who was getting what.

"Damn, I been in here for half the day," I said to myself, as Tyler, Penny, and SK walked into the kitchen.

"Let me know what you need, Tyler," I said.

"I have a order for ten hard and four coke right now," he answered.

"Grab them right there and them. That's $394,000 coming back to us," I said, doing the math in my head.

"Let me get ten and ten," Penny said, rubbing his hands together.

"Coo, that's $710,000 coming back from you," I said.

"I will drop that bread off to you later on tonight after I handle my business," Penny said, grabbing his order.

While Tyler and Penny were walking out the house, Sade's cousin was walking up.

"What's the deal, big cuz?" he said, giving me a hug.

"Hey, lil cuz. I ain't on shit, just trying to get this money," I responded, shutting the door behind him.

"I'm with you on that money tip. I'm always down for getting some money," he said, opening his duffle bag and dumping stacks on the table.

"How much money is this?" I asked, looking at all the blue faces on the table.

"$800,000 but I owed y'all $100,000 on the back sheet," he said.

"You know we weren't tripping about you. You always come correct with your shit. What you want this time around?" I asked.

"I need sixteen coke, four hard, twenty pounds of that Katie, and eight pounds of kush. The remaining cash, buy you a pair of heels," he said, doing the math in his head, as he grabbed his order.

After he left out the house, I went into the back room to the shoe rack that hung on the closet door. Pulling the shoe racks opened up the wall inside the closet. SK came in right behind me, carrying some of the dope and placing them inside the wall.

The house we were using as the stash house looked like someone stayed there. We had beds, TVs, clothes, and food in the house. The only people that knew of this house were Tyler, Penny, and Sade's cousin, Trouble. So, we weren't worried about anyone trying to come in and steal anything from us. We stashed the rest of the dope and closed up the wall.

"I'm tired as hell, baby," I said, hugging SK.

"I can tell you are. You smell," he said, holding his nose and laughing.

"Fuck you! I don't smell, boy. I could not wash this pussy for two days and still niggas will want to smell it," I said, faking mad.

"I'm just playing, baby."

"Nigga, I'm not mad. I just really miss the girls and know if they were here with us, the other day, everything would have played out different, and we would have got that nigga," I said.

"I sent one of my guys through that block to check to see if the van was still sitting on the block, and it was, so I had him secure that money we gave them, but I sent it to their peoples to help them out. I couldn't leave them like that because they went inside that house on business, dropping shit. Let's get out of here," SK said.

"I love you, baby," I said, kissing his lips.

"Damn, your lips taste good," he said.

Chapter 16

I woke up to the smell of food in the air.

Last night, when we got in the house, I rushed to the shower, then to the bed, and passed out.

I entered the kitchen and saw SK making a lovely breakfast. He had the table set for both of us. I also saw two suitcases by the front door like he was on his way somewhere.

"Have a seat, baby," he said, bringing my plate to the table.

"It smell good," I said, digging right into the plate of food.

"Baby, I know you been really missing the girls, so I packed us both suitcases because we goin' to take a trip up to see them for a few days. We going to spend some time out there, and that will give us time to clear our minds, and by this time, your big cousin should have some type of information for you to help y'all out," SK said.

"What about the business?" I asked.

"I rode out to the spot already and dropped loads on Trouble, Tyler, and Penny already, so they would be good while we gone," he said.

***

We were on the highway a few hours later on our way to Chicago to see the girls, and that had me so happy because this was the longest we all had been apart since becoming a team.

The whole time the girls had been in Chicago, we only talked a few times, but I always got updates from Mookie. I knew Mookie was getting tired of me calling for updates, but he didn't know my girls like that, and at any time, something could pop off. But as he put it, they were chilling and were in good hands.

I punched in the address Mookie gave me to where I could find the girls, and the GPS showed us the way.

It took us a few hours to enter into a county called Highland Park. The town was a little less than three hours away from Chicago. When we pulled up in front of the house, there were three cars in the driveway. On the outside, it looked really nice, and with the driveway wrapping around, I knew the inside was big. I kept looking at the cars because I only knew Sade's. We got out the car, and I helped SK roll our suitcases to the door. I rang the doorbell, while we stood on the steps, waiting for someone to open the door for us.

The door swung open, and there stood my sister, Porsche. When she saw me, her eyes popped out of her head. She pointed at me and SK with a smile on her face.

"Bitch! My sister and brother," she yelled, grabbing me and SK around the neck tight. She held us for a minute like it had been years since the last time we saw each other or something.

"Hey, sister," I said.

"Why the hell y'all didn't text or call us to let us know you were headed our way?" she asked me, smiling.

"That look on your face right now. I wanted to see it. Anyway, what's up with y'all in this bitch to the point you haven't let us in yet?" I asked with a little laugh.

"Aww, my bad, y'all. Come on in. Bitch, we ain't been up to nothing. We been out here chilling, looking crazy. Mookie been playing crazy with us with his fat ass. He was supposed to come out here a few days ago to drop off some bud, but since he wanted to keep playing, I had to have my new man toy bring us some," Porsche said.

"Any fool know I don't play games about my weed, so I keep the best with me at all times," I said, pulling out a Ziploc bag full of light green buds.

"Where Sade black ass at?" I asked.

"Come on. I will show you," Porsche said, leading me through the house.

Some brown skinned dude with dreads was in a room playing a game on a big screen as we walked past. He looked up at us when we walked past.

"Who the hell is that nigga in that room?" I whispered.

"That's one of Mookie partners, Lo-Lo. He's the one that be moving all the dope we send up here. He has shit on lock too. I met him the night we went to the club."

I already knew him because I was dealing with him, but now, he had a mouthful of VVs.

When we walked up to Sade's door, all we heard was moaning, so I stopped Porsche from opening the door because I didn't want to see Sade get her back broke in.

"I'm cumming, baby, all over this dick," I heard Sade yell.

"Damn, that was some good sex," the male voice said.

"I'm about to get in the shower for a minute," Sade said.

"Let's give her a few minutes to wash that sex off her, and I will come back," I said, walking back to the front room.

After sitting and listening to Porsche and SK joke for a few minutes, I got up and walked back to Sade's door and knocked.

"What you want, Porsche?" Sade yelled like she was tired of Porsche.

I knocked again, not saying anything.

"Bitch, come in," she said.

I just stood there and continued to knock without replying to her yelling.

"You need to stop playing all the fucking time, bitch. Knocking on people door like you crazy or something," Sade snapped, thinking it was Porsche playing on her door, but when she opened the door and saw me standing there, she was all smiles.

"My sister?" she said, jumping into my arms to hug me just like how Porsche did. "Please tell me you handled that one business, and we can come back home because a bitch is tired of this bullshit. I'm ready to go home. I wish I never promised sister that I would stay down here with her because if it wasn't for the promise, I would have been gone," Sade said.

"Shit isn't over yet, but we on it. We going to stay for a few days to clear our heads, and then, we back on the road to the city. What's up, bro?" I said, looking at Tall, Sade's kids' dad, laying in the bed.

"I'm chilling, had to come through and get my shot. She knew she can't leave a nigga like that, but what's good wit' you?" he asked.

"You know me. I'm good."

"I see y'all bitches been down here living good," I said, pointing at all the shoes and designer bags around Sade's room.

"Yeah, okay, bitch, please! What's the newest that been going on in the city? We been keeping tabs on shit, but we don't know what to believe, but is everything good?" asked Sade.

"Shit is still all bad," I answered, shaking my head, as I thought about everything that went wrong with that team of dudes SK knew.

"What's the update on Tiffany? Is she out yet?" asked Porsche, as I walked back into the living room.

"Naw, they still have her downtown, but she's good. The lawyer said only way they would let her out is if we turn ourselves in, so we have to get shit done. The city called in a lot of help, so they have the ATF, FBI, DEA, and the SWAT is moving around, but I still been hitting the streets. I had to go down to Miami to pick up a shipment, and it was a big order. After we finish this shipment, we could pass the torch and walk away with more than twenty million. But as soon as we hit the city, we goin' to have to move fast. I'm waiting on some information that will help us out, but that's one reason I came down to see y'all because y'all the only ones I trust to get the job done with me," I said.

"Damn, my bad, bro. How are you doing?" Sade asked SK, seeing him there.

"It's all good, but what's good, sis?" he spoke back.

"On another serious note, where the fuck we goin' to sleep at, or do we have to go stay in a hotel for the few days we goin' to be here because we not trying to block y'all with y'all men being here and all," I said.

"Bitch, stop playing games. It's two rooms upstairs," Porsche said, getting up.

Porsche showed us the way to the room we were going to be staying in.

The room was nice and big with its own bathroom, so we were good since we didn't have to share bathrooms.

"We will holler at y'all after y'all get settled in," Porsche said, shutting the door.

When Porsche shut our door, the first thing I did was tear at SK's clothes, lifting his shirt over his head and pulling his Polo jeans down. I dropped down to my knees and slapped his dick in my mouth. I looked up at him and watched, as his head fell back, and his knees started shaking. I didn't want him to nut so fast, so I let his dick slide out of my mouth. I then began to tease the head of his dick with the tip of my tongue. He stood me up and undressed me. We headed to the shower. Stepping into the warm water, it hit our bodies, feeling so good. He bent me over, and I placed my palms flat on the wall in front of me, so we didn't fall. His dick slid right into my pussy.

"Ahh! Ahh! Beat this pussy up because she been bad," I moaned, rubbing my clit super hard.

I knew he would bust fast, hearing me moan and talk nasty, because that was the stuff he liked. His thrusts became harder and harder. Hitting my spot, he had my eyes rolling in the back of my head.

"I'm about to nut, baby," he said, pulling out and nutting all over my ass.

I dropped down to my knees and sucked the remaining nut out of him. We both washed up and got out. That nut was needed because I was backed up.

"Come on downstairs. The food is getting cold." We heard Porsche say outside the door.

"Okay, we will be on our way there in a hot second," I screamed, as we both got dressed.

"This crib is really nice," SK said.

"I was thinking the same thing to myself," I said, as we walked down the stairs into the kitchen to see food on the kitchen table.

When we entered, everybody was at the table, already filling their faces up. The food must have been good because everyone was focused on their plates. We joined them.

"Lo Lo, this is my sister, Queen, and her husband, SK. Y'all know his name since I already said it," Porsche said.

We sat at the table for a few hours, just laughing about old shit or joking on each other. We rolled up some weed and poured a few shots. After a while, we were all ready to lie back and chill with our boos. We all headed to our rooms.

Chapter 17

Special Agent Amber Salt

"Boss, I think we can get at them BBGM girls without Tiffany's help. We just had the best lead we will have drop into our lap," I said to U.S. Attorney Bob Close, as I burst into the office without knocking first.

Bob looked up from his food, hopped up, and rushed to shut the office door, so no one could hear what was being said as I took a seat in front of his desk.

"What is this lead you talking about just dropped in our lap that can help us?" Bob asked me.

"Well, we been watching this dude by the name of Tyler Washington for the past few weeks because he been serving our C.I. dope. The DEA conducted a control buy. I don't know if Tyler Washington's name rings to you, but it should. They call him Ty on the streets, and he's a major dealer in the city and been for years, but we could never get our hands on him. Every time we get near him, he slips through the cracks."

"I heard the name come up in the many circles a few time now that I think about it. But what does he have to do with all this?" Bob asked.

"Well, one of the DEA agents purchased two kilograms of cocaine and one kilogram of heroin from Washington at his house on the south side. The agent posted as a buyer from out of town. We locked Washington up, and he's downstairs in a holding tank screaming that if we help him out on this case, he will give us information that can lead us to the arrest of the BBGM crew. He said he buys his drugs direct from Queen herself. Every time, he goes to some house. He said he knows addresses and names," I said, looking at the smile on Bob's face.

I knew Bob knew this was the break they needed to help their case. He picked up the phone on his desk and dialed a number.

"Hello, this is Bob Close. Can you please have someone go down to the holding tanks and bring up Mr. Washington to my office right away? Thank you and tell them to make it quick," he said, hanging up, smiling hard.

There was a knock at the office door a few minutes later.

"Come on in please," Bob yelled.

Two agents had Washington and ushered him inside the office.

"Please take a seat in that chair, Mr. Washington," Bob said, pointing to a chair next to Agent Amber. "Agents, can you bring us a few cold sodas and a few snacks please because I know Mr. Washington here needs something on his stomach since he been in that holding tank for hours," Bob said.

Bob really didn't give two fucks if Washington ate or not. He just wanted to lay it on thick, so he didn't change his mind. They needed the information he had.

"Can I get these cuffs off me because they hurting my skin?" Washington asked, twisting in his seat.

"Agent Amber, can you please remove all of the restraints, so Mr. Washington will be able to relax while we're talking?"

I removed everything from him because I was in a rush to hear what Washington had to say.

"Now, are you good?" Bob asked.

"Thanks, and yeah, it's all good," he responded, rubbing his wrist.

"Okay, so let me know what business you want with me, Mr. Washington, because my agent already said you been yelling you had some information that could lead to the arrest of the BBGM crew and that them drugs you were selling came direct from Queen herself," Bob said.

"Y'all, all you said is correct," said Washington.

"Mr. Washington, I think you're doing the right thing by coming to talk to us. But overall, this is best for you because with all them drugs and that gun, you're looking at at least fifty years tops, plus you have to think about your past. That would have a big part too, so if you help us, I can assure you that you would be let free in return and no case. I know that sounds better than spending fifty years inside of a jail cell," Bob said.

"I'm not trying to spend another minute in this bitch, so I'm ready to get started on whatever."

Bob went to grab a pen and note pad.

"Alright then, go ahead and let me know who gave you the drugs you were found with, where you meet at to get the drugs, and when did it happen?"

"The other day, I met up with Queen at one of her stash houses where she cooked up a shitload of dope. I sat inside the house for over three hours, waiting on her to finish. She had just got a shipment from her peoples, and all of it was at the stash house," Washington said.

"Here's a few pictures I want you to look at for me please," Bob said, laying them across his desk.

"This picture here is the whole BBGM crew. That's Queen, Porsche, her righthand, Sade, and Tiffany," Washington said, picking up a picture from a party they were at.

Bob and I were so happy. We already knew about Sade from informants who worked with them, but she hadn't done anything for them to arrest her. We had this case at their fingertips and would do anything to keep it that way.

"Tell me how you came in contact with these ladies for them to be going through you to move their drugs," Bob said.

"Well, I only deal with Queen. I haven't heard or seen the rest of them. We been known each other for some time. She dealt with some of the same people I did, so she pulled up on me one day and asked for my help. We already know of each other and knew both names rang bells. She told me she was in some trouble and was hot in the streets, so she laid the plan out to me, and it sounded good. Her plan was that I would serve people for her, and she break me off a percent," Washington said, lying through his teeth.

"When are you able to score from her again?" asked Bob.

"I can score from her anytime I'm ready. All the money has to be correct, then I will text her and meet her at the house on Candle Court on the west side," Washington said.

"Are you willing to make that call and buy from her for us, but we need her to come to you this time?" Bob said. "Do you think she still has drugs in that stash house you were talking about because you did say she just received the shipment the same day you went to that house?" Bob asked.

"Hell yeah, it's dope in that house. It was enough dope to serve every person in the city that sells from big to small. There were at least a few hundred kilos of heroin, crack, coke, and some other shit," Washington said.

"That's good to know. Now, I need the address to that stash house," Bob said.

"I don't know the address, but it's the only red brick house on the block of Candle Court," he said.

Bob grabbed his pen and wrote something in his notebook.

Chapter 18

Queen

We were on our way back to the city from our Chicago trip. Sade and Tall were going to meet us back there. The whole ride, all Porsche did was smile out the window and sing every song that came on. She was acting like she had been gone for months.

It had been almost a week now since the last time I spoke with Cousin Punkin, so I dialed her number and waited for her to pick up.

"Hey, lil' cousin," she said, picking up the phone on the third ring.

"Hey! Anything good came through yet?" I asked her with my fingers crossed.

"As soon as something come through, I got you. I need a little more time, and I got you like I said, but while I'm handling this, you need to keep your hardheaded ass in that fucking house. Also, my connect let me know that the Feds came in and took over y'all case. As we speaking, they all over y'all city, so like I said, stay in the house. When I get that information and give it to you, just make sure you move right with no slip ups this time because this is life or death. They just put you as their leader, so they really don't have anything on you," Cousin Punkin said.

"I hear you and listening too. I will be waiting on your phone call," I said.

"Why you have that look on your face, baby?"

"My cousin said the Feds picked up the case, and they in the city right now. They onto us big time, but she's putting her people to work to get all the information we need to handle our mission, and once we get the information, we need to handle our mission, and once we get the information, we will have to move fast," I said.

"Y'all not worried about the Feds knowing where the new house is?" asked Porsche.

***

Beep! Beep! Beep!
SK's phone let him know he had a text message.

"This is Tyler texting me, saying he has that money he owes, but we have to pull up on him to grab it," SK said.

"How is business going?" Porsche asked.

"It's all good. Right now, the only people we been serving are Tyler, Penny, and Trouble. They been making all type of noise too. We just been in the house chilling," I said.

"So, what we supposed to do, sit back in the house all day, looking at each other?" asked Porsche.

"Nah, bitch, you going to be in the house all day with your feet up, collecting money and helping me come up with a plan, so we can get this bitch ass nigga, Money. So, stop acting so damn silly and get with the program. We running from the Feds right now, so any mishaps can get us killed or life in prison," I said.

We turned down the street, and my heart began to beat fast. Even though the house was in SK's mother's name, there was something about the Feds being around. I made him circle the block twice, just to be safe, because any fool knew the Feds were good at what they did. Everything looked good, so I had him pull up into the driveway. We all got out and rushed in the house. Being home felt so good.

"I'm not trying to drive all the way to the stash house, so I'm goin' to grab a few things we have locked in the safe, then we can go meet up with this nigga, Tyler, at his house," SK said.

While SK went off to do him, I went to grab my gun and my other phone, so I could make a few calls to my peoples who I had making us some fake IDs.

"DaDa, this Queen. You ready for me yet? I been gone for a few days now, so I'm checking on you," I said.

"Pull up on me at the shop and I got you," he said.

"Come on, y'all. Let's get out of here," SK said, leading the way out of the house.

We switched cars and jumped into something lowkey. SK liked the Lincoln truck because it had a stash spot inside that could hold guns or dope.

"Baby, before we meet up with Tyler, I need you to slide past DaDa's shop, so I can pick up them IDs I ordered," I said.

SK pulled over at the curb in front of DaDa's shop.

I dialed DaDa's number and waited for him to pick up.

"Queen?" DaDa said.

"Come outside," I said.

I watched DaDa hang up the phone and excuse himself from the lady he was talking to. DaDa ran a few businesses, and this paint shop was just one of them. Anything you wanted, he was the guy to see. He had connections. He stepped out the shop and looked around. He stood there, staring at the truck, as we sat there, staring at him, for a minute. The windows were so tinted that you had to be in front to see someone inside.

I rolled the window halfway down and called his name. He looked at me and smiled. He opened the back door and jumped in.

"What's good, Queen Bee?" DaDa asked.

"I'm chilling," I responded.

"Man, y'all are the hottest thing in the city right now."

"I know. Pull off, baby," I said.

DaDa was someone I went to school with when I was younger. He had a bald head now, but he used to always fight or have a big knife on him. He was in the streets for years but ended up retiring and opening up a few businesses. He was someone I could always trust. He never tried to talk to me or anything. I had a lot of respect for him.

"DaDa, here's that money," I said, passing a stack of bills behind me.

"And here's them IDs for you," he said. I looked at my ID and handed Porsche hers to check out.

"Damn, these look good," I said, staring at them.

"You already know when I put my stamp on something, it's going to be the best, no matter what."

We pulled back in front of the shop, and DaDa hopped out.

Chapter 19

Tyler

"Y'all need to shut the hell up and listen to what I have to say," Agent Amber said, yelling and clapping her hands loudly to get everyone's attention.

Everybody stopped what they were doing, so they could pay attention to what Amber had to say to them. She was standing in the middle of the floor inside my house where she and a host of other agents had set up, so they could make the bust.

"We just made contact with who we want. She's on her way to the house now as we speak, so we will administer a controlled buy. I need everyone to be in their positions and ready to take her down. Don't nobody move without the okay from me first. Alright, let's get this show on the road and over with the best we can," Agent Amber said as the federal agents all began rushing off to their positions.

I was pacing back-and-forth in the living room, sweating like it was a hundred degrees up in the house. My head hung low, as I thought about what I was about to do to Queen. I was really second-guessing setting Queen up, but my hands were tied, so it was her or me, and I would always put myself first. I also knew I would have to deal with SK after he found out I set his woman up.

"Come on over here so I can tape this wire on you, so we will be able to hear everything y'all are saying, Tyler," Agent Amber said to me from across the room.

"She knows me, and right now, I'm sweating, so I know she going to notice it. I don't know if I can go through with this setup without tipping her off," I said.

"You will get yourself together and get this shit done, or you will spend the rest of your life in prison. Then, you going to be in a cell wishing you had, while they out here balling and having fun. It's about to be showtime, so you need to figure out what you're going to do," Agent Amber said, standing in front of me now.

Damn, it's crazy how life will throw a curve ball because I would have never thought I would be a registered rat for the Feds, I thought.

***

SK

I turned down the block and parked a few houses down from Tyler's, but before I could grab the duffle bag and step out the car, my phone began ringing. It was Penny. This was his third time calling, so it had to be important.

"Are you good, cuz?" Penny asked as soon as I picked up.

"Yeah, I'm good. Why wouldn't I be?" I asked, not understand Penny.

"I thought you knew that while you were gone, the Feds ran up in Tyler crib the other day and locked his ass up. They popped him with some bricks, money, and a gun," Penny said.

"What?! Naw, I didn't know any of this. I just got off the phone with the nigga, and he didn't say anything about any Feds kicking in his door. Matter of fact, I'm sitting down the block from his crib, about to lay something on him and pick up what he owes me," SK said.

"Don't lay shit on that nigga, cuz. It's a setup. You know the game. The Feds even raided the stash house and Queen's old house on 28th Street. He trying to get y'all knocked," Penny said.

"Right on, cuz, for hitting my line and giving me this update. I'm going to handle it. Just stay low and I will get at you later," I said, hanging up and shaking my head.

"Fuck! Fuck! Fuck!" I banged my fist on the steering wheel.

***

Queen

"Baby, what happened? What's goin' on wit' you?" I asked, seeing fire in SK's eyes.

I knew that fire behind them eyes meant trouble for someone.

"Penny just told me that this nigga, Tyler, got knocked by the Feds the other day. The stash house got hit, which I know he gave them the information to do that, and the old house on 28th Street. My own fucking cousin trying to set me up when all he had to do was shut his mouth, and we would have helped his ass," SK said, sounding hurt.

"Fucking rat. I got something for his ass. Pull off and hit English Avenue by school number 28. I know someone who can help us out on handling this, but while I'm in here, talking to him, I need y'all to go grab that duffle bag from Sade's," I said.

I typed the address into the GPS, and we were pulling up ten minutes later. I slid out the car and ran up the stairs to the front door. Before I could knock, the door opened up.

"Queen, how you doing?" asked one of my old friends I used to serve when I was small time.

"I'm doing good these days. Could be better but I'm working with what I have. I need to talk with your son for a few minutes," I said, stepping into the house.

"Bean, someone's here to see you," Stacey yelled.

Bean came from around the corner, looking bad. He was slimmer than the last time I saw him. He used to put in that work but slowed down once the cancer began to spread. Everybody knew he was crazy with that pistol in his hand.

"I know what I'm about to say is going to sound fucked up, but it will help both of us. I need your help, and for your help, it's a million dollars on its way here if you willing to handle this problem for me. It's a dude, that's a few minutes away, trying to set me up with the Feds. He think I'm coming with some dope, so I need you to pull up in front of his crib, and when he get in the car, I need you to bust his head. I'm asking this because I know you only have a few weeks left, and your mother will be good with that million," I said.

Bean stood there in his own thoughts.

"Queen, he's not doing that shit. That shit sound stupid to me," Stacey said.

"Mom, fall back. I'm a grown man, and the plan sounds good to me. At least I can leave you and the kids something," Bean said.

I sat there, happy as hell.

"So, my mother gets the million tonight?" asked Bean.

"My man and sister on their way back with a duffle bag now," I said.

"Well, I'm down. Let me go get ready," he said, rushing back the way he came.

I texted Porsche to see where they were at now. She let me know that they were getting off the highway. A few minutes later, I heard a horn blow in front of the house. I opened the door and waved them inside the house. Stacey sat on the sofa, crying her eyes out, when they walked in the house with the duffle bag.

"Here you go," I said to Stacey, laying the duffle bag on the table and unzipping it, so she could see inside.

Her eyes popped out of her head when she saw all those blue faces inside.

Bean walked back in the room and was shocked to see I had all that money in front of his mother. He walked up to her, hugged her tight, and kissed her.

"Mom, I love you and make sure you do what's right for your grandkids. Let them know I'm sorry, but I had to make sure y'all were good," Bean said, kissing her again.

We left to pull up on Tyler's block. We planned to sit half a block down, just so we could watch.

Chapter 20

Tyler

My phone started lighting up on the table. I stood there, just staring, scared.

"Answer this phone." Agent Amber picked up the phone off the table to hand to me.

The phone was still lighting up, as I held it in my hand, just looking at it.

"Answer it! Damn it!" yelled Amber.

"What's good, Queen?" I answered.

The agents sat around the living room, listening to the whole phone conversation.

***

Queen

"I'm about to turn down your block now. Be outside. I'm going to be in a Jeep with tints," I said, hanging up and just watching the block.

I texted Bean and told him it was showtime.

***

Tyler

"She's pulling down the street. Hold your position, I repeat, hold your position. Here's the money," Agent Amber said to her agents and pushed a bookbag full of money into my chest.

When the Jeep pulled up in front of the house, I was just then walking out with a bookbag. I looked up and down the block before stepping to the Jeep. The locks popped.

"What's good, Queen?" I said, getting into the car, but I was shocked to see Bean sitting in the driver's seat.

"Don't look so shocked to see me. Your peoples sent me over to meet you. Everything is good. What you got for me anyway?" asked Bean, as he began to pull off down the block.

"This is um, huh, five hun'd stacks," I mumbled.

***

Bean

I shook my head, as I watched Tyler. I saw the wire under Tyler's shirt and smiled. His shirt was so tight that I didn't understand how he thought he could get away without anyone noticing. Tyler had the bookbag on the floor, trying to unzip it, and when it opened, he looked up, but when he did, he was staring down the barrel of a .357.

***

Special Agent Amber Salt

"They on the move right now down the block. What should we do, boss?" asked one of the agents.

I stood in the house, trying to come up with the best decision because I wasn't planning on Queen sending someone else or them pulling off.

"Let us know what's the plan, boss, because the Jeep is at the corner, about to turn off the block. Over!"

"Move on them now. Take the Jeep down," I yelled.
Boom! Boom! Boom!

***

Bean

I shot Tyler in the face three times, splattering blood all over the car and himself. I opened the door and pushed Tyler's body out of the car. Out of nowhere, agents came from between houses. Two police Chevys bent the corner and was headed toward the Jeep at full speed. I pressed the gas, and the tires screeched as the Jeep bit down and sped off. The agents opened fire on the Jeep, as it began to take off.

Boom! Boom! Boom! Boom!

Shots riddled the Jeep, rocking it back-and-forth. I ducked low until I was clear of the bullets, then I sat back up.

***

Special Agent Amber Salt

"Whoever in that Jeep driving is crazy," said the agent who was behind the wheel of one of the Chevys.

"Do not let that Jeep get away from us!" I yelled over her radio. "Fuck! Fuck!" I said, rushing out the house and sliding into my F-150 and joining the other agents in the chase.

The driver was doing sixty miles per hour. He shot past a police cruiser that was sitting at the light. The police cruiser threw on its lights and joined the chase. He opened that Jeep up to top speed, as he went down the ramp heading to the highway. I could see him looking in the rearview and seeing that we were on his ass. He started sideswiping every car he passed, hoping it would cause a jam, but I stayed on the Jeep. I was determined to get whoever it was behind the wheel of the Jeep.

***

Bean

I knew it would be hard to get away on the highway, so as I came up to the Martin Luther King exit, I was going to try my luck, but when I looked up in the sky and saw the news was following me also, I knew it was really over with. I picked up my phone and dialed Queen's number.

"What's up?" I said, firing up a blunt.

"Thank you," she said.

"Just make sure my moms is cool. Help her with that money for me and let the streets know who held you down," I said, hanging up. I then called my mother.

"Momma, I love you and make sure you do something good with that money," I said with tears forming in the corner of my eye.

"I love you too. Where are you at?" she asked.

"Turn your TV on and go to channel 59," I said.

She flicked her TV to 59. There was a helicopter hovering over my Jeep, following me with what looked like every police in the city behind him.

"So, where you going, son?" she asked, feeling helpless. I knew she knew I was just doing this to help out the family, but she still didn't want to believe it.

"I'm goin to hell, Momma. I will not spend the last days of my life in some white man's prison. But I was just calling to holler at you one last time and to let you know I loved you," I said, swerving out of the way of a spike strip the police slid across the highway. I had made it all the way toward the mall. I could see that the police were tired of playing games with me because they set up a roadblock. I stopped in the middle of the highway. Some of the police climbed out of their cars and began to walk toward the Jeep.

"Please step out the car!" ordered an officer.

When they were close enough, I hopped out, blasting my .357 and 9mm. Every police officer out there began to fire on me.

***

Bean's body slumped to the ground, and police inched toward his lifeless body.

"What a tragedy…" the news anchor reported.

Bean had made history that night.

"The suspect, Bean Davis, has just been killed by officers after a thirty-minute chase throughout the city. Again, from DMV records, Bean Davis has been killed by officers on the highway. What a tragedy."

Stacey, Bean's mother, sat there, in her living room, in tears, as she watched everything unfold and her son's body lay there on the ground on the highway. She fell to her knees and cried her soul out. This wasn't how he was supposed to pass away. Her phone started ringing nonstop, and she already knew it was people trying to figure out what the deal was, but she didn't want to talk or see anyone at that moment. She looked at the money on the table and knew two things. One, she had to get it out the house before the Feds got there because they were coming, and two, she had to make sure she put some money up for her two grandkids. She didn't know how they were going to take the news, but she was there for them and their mothers.

Chapter 21

SK

When we saw Bean push Tyler's body out of his Jeep, we backed up the street and headed toward our stash spot to check things out. As we rode past the house, we could see a few windows boarded up. The front door was kicked in, but you could still see Porsche's cousin inside the house, cleaning up the mess the Feds left behind. We weren't worried about anyone seeing us since the tints on the truck were so dark that someone would have to open the door to know we were sitting inside.

"Baby, since the Feds don't know you, can you please get out and take this money up to Porsche's cousin? Let her know to get windows and doors fixed, and she can do whatever with the rest," Queen said, handing him a stack of money out of her purse.

I hopped out and walked up to the front door and knocked on the board. We talked through the window for a few minutes until she came outside from the back.

"Again, how you doing, Miss Lady? I'm SK, and Queen's my wife. Don't look fast but her and Porsche is in the car. They know about the Feds coming through and tearing the house up. They both sorry and want you to have this money to fix whatever and the rest go to you and them kids," I said.

"Thank you and can you please thank them for me?" she said, blowing a kiss toward the truck.

"I will do that. Be safe," I said, walking to the truck.

***

Queen

"Now that this nigga tried to set me up with the Feds, I don't know what he told them people or if they did a background check on me and my moms. If they did, we can't go back to our crib because it will pop up as my mom's," SK said.

I picked up my phone and called Mrs. Sunday, the old lady that stayed next door to us.

"Hello, Mrs. Sunday, this is Queen, the lady that stay next to you," I said.

"Yes, I know who you are. What's the matter, child?" she asked.

"I was calling to ask if you seen anyone snooping around our house today?" I asked.

"No, child. Today is like every other day. Queen, is something wrong?" asked Mrs. Sunday, sounding concerned.

"Everything's fine. I was just checking because I heard that some young boys been going around, painting on houses," I said.

"Okay then, child! Make sure you stop to see me when you can," she said before hanging up.

"What she say?" Porsche asked.

"Everything is good at our house. She said the normal been going on."

"If that's the case, he didn't give them my last name, but why set us up when he knew the outcome?" SK asked.

"I know we need to hurry up and move because we have to get them drugs and money at that stash house before we be looking crazy when it's too late," I said.

We made it to the house, got dressed for the task at hand, and were right back out the door, but this time, we were riding inside a van.

I had SK back the van up in the driveway of the house next door to our stash house. I knew the landlord. He was good peoples and got weed from us all the time. He even gave me a spare key to the house, so we walked inside like we belonged in there. We hit a few lights, and we were out the back door in no time. We ducked low as we crossed over the yard but stopped to make sure everything was good to go. Everything seemed to be normal, so we crept up to the back door and headed into the kitchen. Once we got inside the house, we checked every room to make sure.

The house was a mess.

"We good, y'all?" I asked.

"Yeah," both answered.

I grabbed the first bag I saw laying around the house then made it to the bedroom. I pulled on that rack, and the wall opened up, revealing our stash. I began filling up the bag with dope, as Porsche and SK did the same thing with the bags they had. It took us four trips to get all the dope and money to the van. We still had to grab up all the guns in the house. I went to the kitchen, flicked a switch, then turned the knob on the oven, which made the countertop raise up in the air, revealing all our guns. I filled the bag I had with all the extra clips, bullets, and handguns, while Porsche and SK grabbed the bigger guns we had. With the guns over our shoulders, we were out the same way we came. I had to call Sade since we hadn't heard from her.

"Hello?" she answered.

"Bitch, what's up?" I asked.

"Fucking with the kids. What's good?"

"Ask Tall if we can rent out one of his houses, so we can have a stash spot."

"Hold on." She put the phone down. After a few seconds, she picked the phone back up.

"I'm back. I just texted you a address wit' the code to the door," she said.

"So much have happened today, it's crazy, girl," I said.

"Did y'all get to watch the news?" she asked.

"Did I! I saw that shit firsthand."

"I should have known, fucking wit' you, bitch," she said.

"Well, I will update you on everything later, but right now, we need to get to that house, so we can dump all this shit we got. Let bro know I'm about to pay to rebuild some shit inside the house but he won't know," I said.

"It's all good. Do you over there, sis, because I run this shit over here."

"Okay, say that then, ho," I said, hanging up.

We were able to make it to the stash house with no problems. We ended up stashing everything but the money because fucking with Tyler's bitch ass, we lost $700,000, but it was all good. I thought about that million we spent to get his ass, and I smiled. I couldn't wait to get home. It had been a long, stressful day for us. I was going to check on Stacey in a few days because I knew she was going through it bad right now, and she would need all the support. We pulled into our driveway, and we all grabbed a bag of money then headed inside the house. I was so happy when my feet hit the carpet.

Chapter 22

Tiffany

"Y'all need to find y'all something to do and stop hitting our fucking bars because we trying to get us some rest," I yelled.

The deputy that worked that floor stood on the catwalk outside the bars in front of my cell, knocking his keys on the bars.

"Like for real, get the fuck on somewhere and find you something to do."

A few other females on the unit screamed, mad that the deputy woke them up out of their sleep.

"Bitch, you a cop killer. Get the fuck up and get yourself together because you about to be moved in a little while so be ready when I come back," the deputy said.

"What the fuck he mean I'm moving?" I said out loud for everyone to hear her.

"Girl, them police are on bullshit with you because they don't do moves at all around this time of the night," one female yelled from down the range.

"It's 2.34 a.m. I never seen anything like this out of all the years I been getting locked up," another female yelled.

They had me housed in the old side of the county jail in a deadlock block where they only let one person out at a time to shower, use the phone, and whatever else they wanted to do in an hour, like exercise or something. I was happy to be in a deadlock block because I already knew that every deputy hated my guts. Even though they knew I didn't pull the trigger, it just didn't matter to them. It had been days since the last time I ate anything, and with me not wanting to ask any of the other girls for stuff, I just shook it out. The only thing I did was drink a lot of water. Queen had someone bring something the other day for her to eat. Ever since I had walked in the county, my stay had been hell.

Every deputy that came across me expressed the hate they had toward me. I had been treated lesser than a dog, and I knew they had been putting stuff in my food to get back at me.

The same deputy appeared back on the catwalk and beamed his light inside my cell.

"Roll her door. Let's go," he said, walking toward the front slider door.

I walked to the main door where they cuffed me up and walked to the elevators. The whole ride on the elevators, my stomach did flips because I had no idea where I was going or what was happening, but I knew whatever it was, it wasn't good.

Down in the basement, standing at the desk, were two FBI agents dressed in black suits. The deputies turned her over to the FBI agents who immediately started putting chains and bracelets on her.

"We're here on the behalf of the United States," one of the men said.

"Where are y'all taking me?" I asked, my stomach still flipping.

The FBI agents never spoke another word to me, shutting down all communication. They let me know who they were, and that was all they were going to give me. They signed the release of custody paperwork, handed them back to the lady, then rushed me to the garage where a waiting van was parked by the door.

After loading me in the back, they rode up the ramp, pulling into traffic. I sat in the back, my mind going one hundred miles per hour, as I watched the light poles and cars go past. I switched my mind to my girls, knowing if they saw me in the back of the van, they would try to pull a mob move to get me out in no time. After a few corners and ten minutes, they were pulling into this rundown building. When I looked at the building, it made my skin crawl.

They parked the van and pulled me from the backseat, escorting me through some doors to another set of elevators. The whole time, the agents had me by the belly chains, making sure I didn't get too far from them.

"Can you please stop pushing me forward? I know how to walk, and the cuffs on my ankle is hurting too bad," I said, feeling the cuts bleeding on my ankle.

The agents didn't give a fuck what I was talking about, as they continued to push me until we made it to the set of elevators. We stepped on and rode up. When we hit the tenth floor, the bell dinged, and they pushed me off and right into an office where U.S. Assistant Attorney Bob Close sat behind a desk.

As I stepped into the office, I saw two other people sitting in there also.

"Thank you! Have a seat," the one they called Bob Close said to the agents.

"Have a seat," the other man said.

I walked over to the only open chair and took a seat. The cuffs were hurting my skin so bad I wanted to cry, but I held it in. I thought they put them cuffs and chains on me tight to fuck with me. When I sat down, my heart sped up because I was scared as hell, but I knew not to speak about anything unless my lawyer was standing next to me.

"How have you been, Tiffany?" asked Bob Close, as he sat there, watching my movement. The other man stared a hole in me also, and this made me even more scared. Now, I was shaking a little.

"My eyes open, so I'm good, but why do y'all have me here inside this building at this time of the morning?" I answered.

"We have you here to show you we're here to help you out, but you have to take this chance to help yourself, and it's only one shot to helping yourself." The other man spoke.

The other person in the office was a female, and she hadn't spoken one word since I stepped in the office.

"Your case has been handed over to the FBI now, and as you know, I'm the U.S. Attorney that's handling the case. You know my name is Bob Close, and these are some of the agents that's assigned to your case."

The agents introduced themselves to me.

"Now that you know all our names, let me tell you that for your case to make it to my desk, it's bigger than what you thought. Your friends been on the streets, digging a even bigger hole for y'all," Bob said.

"What?" I asked.

"With you already being locked up, you can get the best deal on the table because, as of right now, you're facing life in prison. If you don't help yourself, then you will be fucked big time. I hope you know when they get ahold of your crew, one of them will roll on you. It always happens that way. You know that right, Tiffany?" asked Bob.

I just sat there, staring at Bob in the eyes, not saying one word to him. I was trying to see if he was joking, which I knew he was.

"Okay, I should enlighten you. Every officer that was killed when they were arresting you that night falls on your back," Bob said.

My body shook with the statement he had just made, and I could tell Bob saw the look in my eyes. I knew he had been doing this job for over twenty years.

"And, before I forget to tell you, we have you on trafficking drugs, and that could get you the RICO charge. What, you didn't think we knew that shit? We're the Feds. We know everything," said Bob.

"Well, I been listening to everything y'all put on the table for the last ten minutes, so now it's my time to talk, and y'all listen. Grab a pen and paper because I want the world to know this."

"Okay, what is it that I'm writing?" Bob asked, ready to write.

"Tiffany looks at her crew as her sisters, and they have formed a bond that can't be broken, so please stop trying to bend something that's solid. I'm not a rat. Now, get my lawyer," I said.

"You fucking up big time, Tiffany," Bob said, standing up with fire in his eyes.

"Yeah, Tiffany, once you get charged, it will be hard for you to come back and get what we are putting on the table. You still might have to do a little time, but if you work with us now, you will walk right back in the free world in no time and go back to your life. We can give you money, buy you a house anywhere in the world, and protect you. Whatever it is, all you have to do is tell us, and we will make it happen, just work with us," the female spoke.

"This will be your only chance to walk away," said Bob. I knew he wished I said okay to the deal.

"I'd rather face the heat then to help you bitches," I said, smiling.

Bob's eyes flashed red, and his jaw tightened.

"Get her out my fucking office and please let the other agents know to put her in Hell until further notice," ordered Bob.

"What the fuck is Hell?" I asked, as I was pushed out of the office.

All the agents did was laugh at me asking about what Hell was. They pushed me all the way back to the elevators we rode up in. Once inside, one pushed Level L, and a few seconds later, we were on the garage floor. They escorted me back to the van and put me in the back.

"Where am I going now?" I asked, yelling at the agents.

The agents kept driving, not pay attention to anything I was talking about. I continued to yell. After a while, the agent that was driving pulled over to the side and pulled the back door open and stuck a needle into my arm. My eyelids got heavy before they could shut the back door. I heard them say they didn't want to do this to me, but they were tired of me yelling.

When I woke up, the agents were still driving. I started to think the worst. I felt that they were driving farther in the country to kill me just because the other police officers got killed. The agents turned down a road, and it looked like a farm. The van came to a stop, and that was when I saw the small plane.

"That's them right there," the agent who was driving said, as the plane began to stop.

They both got out the van and headed over to the plane and started talking to the pilot. They walked back to the van, laughing, as they opened the back doors.

"Come on. It's showtime. They waiting on you," said one agent.

"Who waiting on me?" I asked.

"The pilot and his partner."

"Why the hell am I getting on a plane?" I asked, refusing to get out the van.

"I'm going to tell you to step out the van one more time, then we going to have a problem," the agent said.

I still refused to budge at their statement.

One of the agents hopped inside the van and began to pull at my chain, while the other one stuck me with another needle and then watched me slump over in my seat. The agents snatched me from the back and carried me to the airplane and helped the Marshals fasten me to the chains. Within seconds, the plane was up in the air, and I drifted off in a deep sleep.

***

Bang! Bang! Bang! Bang!
The female guard hit the keys on my slot.

"Get up and grab food if you want to eat. Bang! Bang! Bang!" she said.

"I'm not eating this shit so shut my slot and go on 'bout your business," I yelled.

"Girl, get up and grab this food. It's from Queen and the girls," the guard said.

I rolled off my bed and rushed over to grab the Styrofoam tray and orange juice. The food smelled so good.

"Thank you. Can you tell me where I'm at because they hit me with something, and I was passed out," I said.

"You in Kansas City. They flew you in early in the morning. You slept all day. They told us they hit you with that sleepy time, so you could get on the plane. You're in the place they call Hell right now," she said.

"That's the second time I heard Hell. What's that all about?"

"You will see for yourself if you stay here long enough to learn why they call it that. But Queen said everything will be good soon, just keep your head up. I don't work this unit but will try to get you some more food for you to eat," the guard said.

"Can you please tell Queen I said they coming for them and to get me out of here asap," I said. jumping after feeling something run across her legs.

"Yeah, I got you, and as of right now, she out there trying to get you out."

"Okay, thank you for the food and tell Queen I said I love them, and they know she has all the dope that the city been buying," I said.

"Well, keep your head up and pray it helps."

"Thank you again," I said before her slot shut all the way.

Chapter 23

Queen

"Queen, you and Porsche going to get fucked up messing with me. What the hell y'all done got y'all self into up there in the city?" Kenya yelled through the phone.

I had to pull the phone away from my ear just so Kenya wouldn't bust my eardrum.

"What you talking about? Why would you ask me that?" I asked.

"Don't sit on this phone and play me like I'm a fool. You know why the hell I'm asking. You should know by now that you can't keep shit from me. My ears are always to the streets, so you will never be able to keep anything from me. Now, why the hell the police kick in the house door? What's going on, Queen? And you better not fix your lips to lie either," said Kenya.

"It's some small shit, but I'm on top of it. I already told you the police was looking for us, but it's all under control," I said.

"Don't make me hop on one of these planes and come up there to fuck y'all up because you already know I will so stop playing with me," Kenya said.

"Calm down, Kenya. I got this shit under control. You just need to stop worrying about what's going on in this city and continue focusing on yourself because I see you looking good on social media," I said.

"I hear you, but when I do come back, I need everything to still be standing like when I left. When I got the call the police kicked in the door, it scared me half to death, thinking about you. You and Porsche can come down here for a while, so we can figure whatever out. That way, I will know y'all are safe and won't get in anymore trouble, and I want to see you."

"We good, Momma. We have to handle this, then we will make that road trip," I said, meaning every word.

"Okay, the program Punkin helped me get into really been helping me out. I haven't smoked since the last time you and I talked, and I don't' want it either. The program is having a party, and everybody is asking their family to be there for support, so I need y'all down here," she said.

Kenya was still staying in Miami with Cousin Punkin, getting herself together, and Cousin Punkin was doing good with helping her out. Kenya had a car and house, and she had even been running one of Cousin Punkin's businesses and was told if she stayed clean for six months, Cousin Punkin would sign it over to her.

"We will be there to see you soon and tell Cousin Pooder I sent that money to her account so get at me when she have some free time on her hands," I said.

"I love you, Queen."

"Love you too and happy you putting in the work to stay clean, Ma," I said, meaning it from the heart.

"Take care of yourself and Porsche please."

"I will, Ma."

Click.

"Ahhh…That was so sweet of you. Sounds like your mother has found her sway back down in the south," SK said, leaning over and kissing my lips.

Me and SK had been in the house, chilling for the past few days, and since SK owned his business, he took a little time off to spend with me. Plus, he was backed up on his college work, so he had to get online and knock his homework out. The whole time we had been chilling in the crib, all we had done was watch TV, fuck, smoke, then eat, and that was the order.

"Yeah, Ma down there doing good for herself, and I'm glad to hear that spark in her voice. I'm glad I sent her down there because if I didn't, I don't know where she would be. Really, I think she should stay down there because it's nothing up this way," I said.

"Whenever you do slide back down to Miami, I will be taking that trip wit' you. We didn't get to do anything last time because it was all about handling business, but this time, I'm trying to turn the city upside down," SK said.

"That's all coo, but in the meantime, let me get some of the good dick," I said, pulling his boxers down.

I laid back in the bed, and SK began feasting on my clit.

"Suck this stress out of me, baby," I moaned while throwing my hips into his face. "Ahhh. That's it, right there... Ahh." I leaned back and closed my eyes.

SK continued to suck, lick, and play in my pussy.

"I'm cumming, baby," I said, cumming all in SK's mouth, as he kept licking it up.

"Damn, you taste sweet," he said, getting into the bed. He put his head into my pussy and held it but pushed the rest in while putting my legs behind my head. Once he got into it, he started pounding on my pussy, hitting my spot.

"I'm cumming again," I said, spraying cum everywhere.

Our moment of paradise was interrupted by the phone ringing after only ten minutes of fucking. My eyes popped open.

"Fuck that phone right now," SK said, digging deeper in my pussy.

"I have to take that call," I said, moaning and not wanting the feeling to stop.

"They will call back," he said, flipping me over, so I could ride the dick.

While riding his dick, I grabbed my cell phone off the nightstand.

"Hello?"

"Queen, it's me," Cousin Punkin said.

"What's up, cousin? Tell me you have something good for me because I need some good news," I said, watching SK's sex face.

"Well, I been sending your little friend food and letting her know it came from you. But the thing is they sent her off to Hell," Cousin Punkin said.

"What's that?" I asked.

"Are you having sex while I'm on the phone?" Cousin Punkin asked.

"No," I lied.

"Well, it's all the way in Kansas. They call it Hell because they have rats the size of cats. They send people down there to break them down. I had my connect to ask her if she was good. My connect said the look she saw in your friend's eyes tell it all, and it's not looking good. She ready to break down."

"I'm not worried about her snitching on us. She a solid chick," I said confidently.

"Let me explain something to you, lil cousin. You don't know that girl like that. You did years in prison, came home, and jumped headfirst back in with that girl. All them years you were gone, she could have done a lot of things you don't know of or snitched on thousands of people. Pooder told us once y'all left that she didn't trust that girl because her gut tells her that the girl isn't right, but she let you go because she knew you was going to continue to do whatever you pleased. The type of time y'all facing will bring the hardest nigga down to their knees. In all the years I been doing this, I have seen many people fall weak to the pressure the Feds put on them. Just don't put too much trust into that girl. They can and will break her down. The Feds isn't like the local IPD y'all be dealing with. They on a whole nother level," Cousin Punkin said.

"Did your connect ever get a drop on that other thing we were talking about?" I asked.

"Yes, I have a little something for you. I'm texting all I have to your phone now."

"Thank you, cousin," I said, looking at the information on my screen.

"Give me a call if you need me and or when this shit is handled, so I can help you get out this shit," Cousin Punkin said, hanging up.

Cousin Punkin had gotten Dr. Ross' office and home address. She had times and dates of when Money's mother had to go see Dr. Ross. She even had the new address where they were staying at. She had the daycare name where Money's kids went to school. It was on the south side of town, and it was called Fun Time.

"Mock Martin and Omar Jesus?" I repeated, scrolling down my phone because it didn't add up to me that this bitch, Marilyn, would name her son after my dad. My dad's name was Omar Jesus, but the city started calling him Black Jesus because he always helped people out, no matter what.

Chapter 24

Tiffany

In the past few days, I had only eaten three meals. Each morning when they opened my tray slot, they either threw my tray on the floor, or when I opened it up, it had roaches or rat shit or piss in my cup. One morning while I was mixing up my food, I came across a broken razor. Not being able to eat or get something to drink besides the water out of my sink and with everything going on, it had been taking its toll on my mind and body. I even had to deal with rats that crawled all over me and the floor throughout the day. The rats had been feasting on my body since I walked into that cell. Bite marks covered my whole body, and every time I explained this to the guards, they just laughed at me like it was some type of joke, or they would act like they just didn't give a fuck. I just couldn't get a break.

"Argh! Argh! I'm fucking hungry and tired of these damn rats," I screamed, as I began pulling at my hair while walking in circles.

"You better stop all that fucking yelling in that damn cell before we come in there and give you a reason to be yelling," said one of the guards, as he banged on my door with his keys.

"When will I be able to move out of this cell with these big ass rats?" I asked.

"Yes, you can get moved, but it all depends on you," the guard said, laughing.

"Tell me what it depends on because I need to be moved," I said.

"Depends on what you have to say and who you have to say the shit to," said the guard.

"Can you please go grab the phone, so I can make a phone call?"

"I can go get it, but that all depends."

"Argh! Argh! Depend on what this time?" I asked.

"On who you about to try to call and what you goin' to say to them," he said.

"I would like to get the phone, so I can place a call to my lawyer and ask him a few question I need some answers to."

"Calling your lawyer will not get you on the phone, so you need to think of someone else you may can call," the guard said.

"Well, then fuck my lawyer. I will just hit my father for a few minutes to let him know that I'm doing good because if he don't hear from me, he will start calling the news stations," I said, thinking that would get me the phone faster.

"That was your second wrong answer there, so that mean you only have one more time to get the correct answer, so who would you like to call now?"

"Fuck this weak bullshit. I'm tired of going through this. I want to go home bad," I yelled.

"Well, you know you have one more time to give me the correct answer, so who would you like to place a call to?" the guard asked her again.

"Okay then. Go get that phone so I can call to talk to U.S. Assistant Attorney Bob Close," I said, letting my head down to her chest.

"Third time is a charm because you just made the right choice with that answer," the guard said, walking off from my cell door.

Twenty minutes passed by before the guard came back to my cell with the cordless phone and handed it to me through her food slot. Then, he handed her a business card with Bob

Close's office and cell number on there. I held the phone in my hand for a few minutes before dialing the office number and waiting for someone to pick up.

"This is Bob Close speaking. How may I help you today?" he asked, picking up.

"Mr. Bob Close, this is Tiffany speaking," I said.

***

Bob Close
Hearing Tiffany's name and voice, I sat up in my chair and took my glasses off. I was in the office, working on the BBGM case.

"Tiffany, I see! How have you been? You like your stay down in the Hell Box?" I asked, laughing.

"Ain't shit funny. You know damn well I haven't liked this place," said Tiffany.

"Well, you did it to yourself."

"When can I get out of this place and come back to the city or go home to my loved ones?" she asked.

"You can go home anytime. It all depends on you and what you are willing to do to make that happen for yourself," I said.

***

At that moment, I was tired of hearing the word depends. I stood in the middle of my cell and began to pull at my hair again because I didn't know what to do.

"It all comes down to how had you wanna go home to your loved ones, Tiffany," said Bob. I could hear in his voice that he knew my stay in the Hell Box was taking its toll on my mind. I was sure they built that building just for this purpose alone.

"I want to go home so bad because this place is driving me crazy. I haven't ate anything in days."

"Well, you know what the hell I want from you, so are you willing to give up the BBGM crew?" asked Bob.

"So, all I have to do is give you all the information I know about them, and I can go home?" I asked.

"If I find your cooperation to be one hundred percent truthful, I will recommend to the judge that he consider giving you a lower sentence, and you can be on your way home," Bob said.

"Okay, I'm willing to cooperate and give all the information I have," I said.

"This case is getting very serious. If you wasn't willing to help yourself, you would have been fucked in the long run because it's only a matter of time before we arrest your friend group. So, are you ready to come back and talk with me?" asked Bob.

"I been ready to talk with you."

"Well then, I will send for you soon. Tiffany, you already know what is expected of you once you step foot inside my office. There will be no games played. Do you understand me?" asked Bob.

"Yes, I understand clearly," I said.

"I'm telling you now, Tiffany, if you don't come to play ball with me, then I will send you deeper in the Hell Box. You think you having a hard time now…"

"I said I understood you, so you don't have to keep talking about the shit," I said, snapping at Bob.

"Alright then. I'll see you soon and have a nice trip."

Click.

I set the phone on my food slot and went to lay down on my bunk. *Am I making the right choice?* I thought.

"You know you just made the right choice for yourself and family," the guard said, shutting the slot and walking off.

"Fuck you, bitch," I screamed.

The guard walked back to my door and popped my food slot back open.

"I might be a bitch, but you'll never see me sell out any of my friends. You a rat, just like the ones inside your room," he said, laughing.

I laid on my bunk and stared at the wall, thinking about all the guard had just said to me. I knew in my heart that if the shoes were on the other foot, none of the girls would have done this to me, but I wasn't as strong as them. I also knew that years from now, people wouldn't even be thinking about me becoming a rat.

Chapter 25

Tiffany

A few days later, in the middle of the night, the guards came to escort me down to the main floor where two Marshals were waiting on me. U already knew the program, so I turned with my hands behind my back, so they could put the chains on me.

I was so happy to be getting out of that place that I wore a smile on my face. Getting out of there meant I was a step closer to going home as the Marshals drove the van to a private airport. This time around, I was rushing to get on the plane. As I sat in my seat, I looked out the window and thought, *I'm on my way home.*

An hour and a half later, the plane touched down in Indianapolis, and as the door opened, there were two police vans waiting on me. The same two that drove me the first time were waiting.

"Come on, get the hell up in the van," one of the Marshals said, not thinking about helping me step up. Once I got seated, they shut the door, hopped in, and sped off.

It took them thirty minutes to get me to the destination.

***

Bob Close

I stood by the door, as the van pulled into the building and parked. I couldn't wait to get Tiffany out the van and see what she had to say. With her being a part of the crew, I knew she had some deep things to tell me.

"Thank y'all. I have it from here," I said, taking a hold of Tiffany's belly chains and walking to the elevators. We stepped on, and I pressed the third-floor button. When the doors opened, she was led back to my office.

"Please have a seat, Tiffany," I said, walking around and taking one of my own.

As I sat in front of Tiffany, waiting for her to speak, I could barely contain himself.

"Let's get down to business because time isn't on either of our sides. With that said, I need to know everything that's on your mind," I said.

***

Tiffany

Sitting in front of Bob, at that moment, I started thinking about what I was about to do to my girls, and it made me feel bad, but when the thought of spending the rest of my life in prison popped in my mind, all of that other stuff went out the door. I wasn't going to spend the rest of my life in a prison and do what she was told to do all day long.

"Well, I want to know every little detail. How you became part of they crew? Who is the boss? Stuff like that," Bob said.

"I knew Queen first. She went to high school with me back in Miami for a while. I guess she came to stay with her cousin because she had been in some type of troubles here in Indianapolis, so her mother sent her down to Miami where we met. My dad stays in Miami, and that's who I was staying with. Well, one day, me and Queen hooked up after she beat some girl up and had to run away from the police. Speeding along the story, my dad and I was coming to Indianapolis to see my mother, so I told Queen, and she asked to take the trip with us, which my dad said yes to. After that day, I didn't see Queen for years til she popped up over my father's house

119

with a duffle bag inside her car with $150,000 inside. We talked for a little while, and I found out she just came home from prison, then she asked if I wanted to come back here to make some money," I said.

"What was the plan for how y'all was going to get some money?" Bob asked.

"We were going to sell drugs to get money."

"Who is we, and where were the drugs coming from in the first place?"

"When I say we, I'm talking about BBGM," I said.

"I see you keep running around who y'all was scoring y'all drugs from."

I knew that once I told them where the drugs were coming from, my dad was going away for a very long time. I didn't want to see my father behind bars because of me, but I wanted to go home bad at the same time.

"I'm telling you now, Tiffany, if you play any games and hold back on me, you're done, so make sure you think long and hard on what you want to do. So, again, who were y'all scoring y'all drugs from?" Bob asked again.

Taking a deep breath and rolling my eyes at the same time, I said, "We were scoring our drugs from my father, Roast."

Bob began to write some notes down on his yellow note pad.

"Who is Roast?" asked Bob.

"My father was a old school player in the city back in the day, but now, he stays in Miami," I answered.

"Are we talking about the Roast that used to run around this city with the WSF back when they had the streets on lock? Money was flowing then," Bob said.

"Yes, that's my father, and he still have money flowing."

Bob sat there for a hot second. He knew if he played this right, he would be able to take Roast and the BBGM down all together. He had been trying to slap cuffs on Roast since back in the day, but he always slid through, and the last time, he left and became a ghost. He knew that with both cases, he could take his career to the next level.

Chapter 26

SK

After looking over all the information she received from her cousin, Punkin, Queen handed everything over to me, so I could look over it before having to come up with something.

I paid his guy, Lil' Nate, a visit at his carwash on 42nd and Post Road. When I pulled into the parking lot, it was packed, so I parked and walked right into Lil' Nate's office.

"What's good, nigga?" Lil' Nate said, as soon as he saw me.

"Shit, chilling. I came to holla at you about something that's important," I said, sitting down.

"I'm all ears," Lil' Nate said.

"Look, here's $150,000 in cash. I need a job done, but it have to be done right. All I need done is for someone to watch this school/daycare where this man here will be dropping off his sons every day. I need you to write down everything you see every day. Also, write down every car they pull up in," I said, laying pictures on Lil' Nate's desk.

"Brother, if you want the nigga done, you know my shooter is nothing but a call away. They would light that whole block up without thinking twice."

Lil Nate was a goon to no end. He grew up on the far east side of Post Road. He did a bid and came home to take shit over.

"Naw, bro, them the Feds you watching. The nigga is trying to take down my wifey by getting on the stand, so we don't want that type of heat on us. You feel me?" I said.

"Well, I got you."

***

Queen

Late last night, Lil' Nate pulled up on us and dropped all the information he had taken notes on. He also surprised us when he told us he met one of the teachers and took her out to dinner the night before. When he told us that, I knew we were going to get away with this mission.

Me, SK, Porsche, and Sade sat outside the school/daycare a block up, just watching things for ourselves behind dark tints. Everything Lil' Nate took note off was on point and correct. The Feds stood out like sore thumbs. As we sat there, watching, we passed the blunts back-and-forth and laughed at them. The Feds always thoughts they were slick, but really, they were playing themselves. We continued to watch the school/daycare like clockwork. Right on time, Money, his mother, and the boys stepped out of the Cadillac truck, and they all walked into the building.

"I don't think it's a bad thing to let Lil' Nate team handle this job. Them little niggas ain't nothing to play with," Porsche said from the backseat.

"Leaving shit up to you, we will keep on building cases on ourselves. We need that nigga alive because I need answers, plus he thinks shit is sweet," I said.

It had been over a week since I received all that information from Cousin Punkin. We were just waiting on the right time to put our plan together.

Money and his mother exited the building, all smiles. He looked up the block, and I could have sworn we made eye contact, but he ducked low into the truck, and then, they sped off.

"We know on Fridays, they drop Money's mother off at Dr. Ross' office before they spin to drop the boys off at school. I think next Friday, we should move on them. I feel we should take this week, spend it together, have a little fun just in case shit don't pan out like we want it. I have money split up for us all. Lawyers is waiting so we good," I said.

"So, what's the plan?" Sade asked.

"SK, your cousin still works for UPS?" I asked.

"Yeah, why, what's up?" he asked.

"I need you to drop a few dollars on him. That way, we can borrow his truck and outfit for a few hours. Now, I'm goin' this way because, when you park that UPS truck, I want you to block the Feds truck in then walk into the school with a few boxes and just watch Money's every move. We know after he sign the boys in, he wait for the teacher to come and get them to put them in the breakfast line. That's where you come in at, Sade. You going to play as a teacher, and when you see the boys, you get them back out of line and bring them out the side door since we know that the Feds wouldn't be on that side of the building. Once the boys are out the office, I want you to stop SK and show him your phone, which Porsche would have his mother already tied up," I said.

"So, you telling me, you think with all the Feds around the building, that Money's going to just walk out with us, knowing what type of people we are?" asked Porsche.

"Hell yeah, he going to come after we show him his mother and boys. He know we not playing, so he will play by our rules. Watch and see. The nigga is a pussy, and it makes me sick that I used to want him so bad," I said.

"Porsche, you just make sure you ready and don't fuck shit up at Dr. Ross' office next week. Be there hours beforehand because everything is about time," Sade said.

"Okay, baby, I see you thought this shit out," SK said, kissing my lips.

"Yeah, the whole time we been sitting here, I been putting it together. Anyway, how are we looking in the streets because I see you been dropping loads off into that safe?" I said to Sade.

"Bitch, with the help of SK, we stepped up a little and doing good. I just pick up money. The rest is all SK doing."

SK's phone lit up, letting him know he had a message. He picked up the phone and began to read the message out loud.

"Bro, this Lit' Nate. I need you and wifey to pull up on this soul food place on 71st out north. I'm taking that teacher there and think y'all should get y'all own feel of her. Just in case shit do come together, just bring a few bands with you. That way, she will know we come in good faith." SK finished reading.

"Well, let's drop these bitches off and grab some money," I said.

"Can y'all bring me some food back?" Porsche asked, as SK pulled off.

"All you want to do is smoke, shoot guns, and eat. Damn, ho," I said.

***

Bob Close

I sat behind my desk, sharing all the information I had received from Tiffany the other day. Amber sat there, listening with a smile so bright she could have lit up a dark street. With every word I spoke, Amber moved around in her chair. She could hardly conceal her excitement. She knew from the jump that helping me out on this case would help her career.

"Do you know Roast's still been working from Miami to Indianapolis? I had him before, but every time, he got away. I let his case die down because after the last time, he just never showed his face again. His name didn't even pop up until now. We were investigating him for a while, but it all stopped," I said.

"This the same Roast we were investigating too?" Agent Amber asked.

"Yeah, it's the same one. I'm trying to put a plan together where we can knock both Roast and BBGM crew at the same time. We're talking about international crimes being committed here," I said.

"If Tiffany's willing to fully cooperate with us, we can add Roast to our investigation. Then, we'll be able to connect the dots to all kinds of criminal enterprises – some criminal enterprises we may not even know exist."

"Let's get the ball rolling then," I said.

Chapter 27

Lil' Nate

By the time nightfall hit, me and Karen were cruising through the city, getting to know each other better. We were set to meet SK and Queen in an hour. Karen was driving, so she showed me where she grow up at. We connected on so many levels that it had both of us a little scared. She pointed out things, as she rode on the south side. All I did was nod my head to the words she spoke.

"Now this is my type of surrounding," I said while watching niggas and bitches hog the block, doing them.

She continued to drive up East Street. "My dad owned them two cribs, but my aunt took over them when he got killed, then my uncles and my brother turned them into dope and weed spots. Is it coo if I swing by my friends' crib?" she asked.

"I'm riding with you, sweetheart," I said. She hit a few corners then pulled up into the driveway of a nice, small house.

"Come on. Let's go in," she said, getting out and walking into a smoke clouded house.

"Damn, that smells like that good shit," I said, liking this side of her. She was a woman but still hood all in one, and that was what I loved.

"Hey, Karen," her friend said, hugging her.

"This is my friend, Nate."

"Nice to meet you. My name is Sherry," she said, extending her hand for a shake.

"Likewise," I said, shaking her hand.

"Nate is trying to buy some of that good shit," Karen said.

"Hold on one second," Sherry said, walking off toward the back. When she came back into the room, she tossed me a sandwich bag with buds in it.

"How much you want for this?" I asked, looking at the lime green buds.

"That's like ten grams of Apple Twist I just got in the other day. Give me $200," Sherry said.

"Well, we have to be going. I will call you later tonight," Karen said as soon as I slapped $200 in Sherry's hands.

We hit the highway and listened to some slow jams as we rode to the soul food place.

Thirty minutes later, we were pulling into the parking lot of Wylosha's Soul Food.

While Karen fixed her hair and put on her lipstick, I walked around to the driver's side and opened her door, so I could help her out the car. She held his arm tight as she strutted like a super model as we walked into the restaurant. I looked around to see if he spotted SK and found him sitting in the back with a bad chick.

"My cousin is sitting in the back over there," I said, pointing.

The hostess led them to the table, and once I got there, I saw that it was Queen who was sitting with SK. She looked different.

"Karen, this is my cousin, SK, and his lady, Pam." I introduced the table.

"Hello, both SK and Pam," Karen said.

Queen was glad that Lil' Nate used a name other than her real one.

"So, how you two meet?" Queen asked.

"Well, Nate was at the same store I shop at, and I needed some help carrying my bags," Karen said.

"That was sweet of you," Queen said.

"Me and Pam met on a business trip. We both just had a nasty breakup, and just so happened, we were sitting next to each other, and two years later, we still going hard. I thank God every day for this blessing," SK said, kissing Queen.

"What type of businesses you have?" Karen asked.

"I have my own security business, and Pam does hair."

***

Queen

"What is it that you do?" I asked.

"I'm a teacher. The pay is trash, but I love kids," Karen said, her eyes lighting up.

"That's good. We need more teachers, and they need to start paying more because the kids are our future. What age?" I asked.

"I teach ages four to five."

"Not trying to count your pockets, but how much does teachers make a year?" SK wanted to know.

"I will say no more than $50,000 a year, and that's bad," Karen said.

"Cuz, Karen surprised me tonight. She showed me where she was from and everything. I'm going to have to show her how I get down too soon. She from the hood and understand us more than what we think," Lil' Nate said.

Karen slapped Lil' Nate on the arm. "I didn't want them to know I'm from the hood."

"Girl, it's okay because everyone at this table is from the hood, but that's neither here or there. Let's hit the lady's room, so the guys can talk for a little while," I said, getting up and heading toward the restroom with Karen following me.

"How long have you and Lil' Nate been knowing each other?" Karen asked, looking at herself in the mirror.

"That's my man's people. He a good dude and seems to really like you," I said, checking the stall to make sure no one else was inside.

"I really like him too."

"Since we're in here alone, let me get to the point of asking you to step in here. I have a problem, and you can help me out a long way. I have $75,000 right here in my bag for your help," I said, showing Karen the stacks of cash.

"What type of problem, and did Nate know about this?" Karen asked, feeling like she had been setup.

"No, Nate didn't know about this. But when he told my mans who you were, we did a background check, and it so happens that you the piece we need to this puzzle. You said it yourself. You only get about $50,000 a year. I'm about to pay you $75,000 cold cash," I said.

"You never did say what type of problems you were having."

"Well, I'm trying to get a hold of my little cousins that attend your school and somehow get them out the building," I said.

"That's it for $75,000?" Karen asked.

"Yeah, there is nothing more."

"I'm with that shit," Karen said, smiling.

"This is my plan," I said, putting my plan on the table for Karen.

"That won't work at all because they keep a Fed inside a classroom that watch that side of the building. Also, I thought you were only trying to get your little cousins, and if you add another $25,000 to that $75,000, I will give you a plan that will get you what you want," Karen said.

"Come on, let's go back to the table, so you could tell us all the plan at the same time," I told Karen.

"Okay, Pam told me the problem y'all are having, and I'm willing to help y'all out, but the plan y'all had set isn't going to work at all, but that UPS delivery thing will though. This is what y'all need to do," Karen said, putting down the plan.

I was all smiles as I listened to the plan. I was liking Karen but knew I couldn't trust her just yet.

"Are you sure you down for this, sweetheart?" Lil' Nate asked, playing his role.

"Hell yeah, I'm sure. She giving me $100,000," Karen said, looking at Lil' Nate like he was crazy.

"Y'all going to need one more person to help y'all out," Karen said.

Me and SK both looked at Lil' Nate. He sat there, wearing a smile on his face.

"Y'all know I'm with the shits," he said.

"Then it's all set," SK said.

"Let's eat then."

Chapter 28

Lil' Nate, Sade, SK, Porsche, and myself sat in the basement of our home.

"I called all of you over, so I could talk to y'all. Girls, this is Lil' Nate. He helped with this new plan. He have this teacher he's fucking that works inside the school. I let her know my plan, and she was like they keep a Fed inside a classroom on that side. Anyway, Porsche, you continue with grabbing his mother from Dr. Ross' office. Sade, the teacher Lil' Nate is fucking is going to show you this secret door in the basement that leads to the building next door to the school. They don't use it anymore. She going to usher you and the kids to this door where I will be waiting on y'all. Then, I need you to rush back inside to grab Money from Lil' Nate," I said.

"It's a bathroom right across from the main office. I'm going to be inside, watching from there. Karen will knock on the door on her way to bring you the kids, so that gives me about twenty to thirty seconds to grab Money and walk him down the hall," Lil' Nate said.

"What about the Feds that's already in the building?" asked Porsche.

"Well, she told us about the one in that classroom and two that sits inside her classroom, but by the time she do her calls, we will be long gone," I told them.

"So, does everyone know what's going on because I'm tired of this shit? We move at 7 a.m. because school starts at

8 a.m., and we have to be there beforehand to all get in place," SK said.

"We all good, bro. Next Friday," said Sade.

***

For that whole next week, we had a ball. We went to Miami to see Kenya for a day then hit New York and then Cali before heading back to the crib. Time went past fast.

Lil Nate stayed the night over in the basement, as Sade and Porsche slept in their rooms upstairs. Around 6 a.m., Porsche woke everyone up with breakfast because we had to be out the door at 7 a.m.

Porsche loaded inside her van, as the rest of us, besides Lil' Nate, hopped in our truck. I had to take SK to meet his peoples like ten minutes from the school, so he could grab that outfit and truck.

As we began to pull off, I lit a fat ass blunt up, so I could get my mind right. This had to go as planned. My phone lit up with Porsche calling.

"Hello?" I picked up.

"This time, sis, you can't spare that weak ass nigga," she said.

"Girl, we talking about life or death. I got this shit," I said, hanging the phone up in her ear.

We pulled up to where Karen told us to meet her at. She had spare keys to the building's door. Sade hopped out at the same time as Lil' Nate and walked toward where Karen was waiting. It was only 7:42 a.m., so the parents and school buses should be pulling up in the next ten minutes.

Once Karen had them inside the building, she would tell them where to go before walking to where all the teachers stood. I pulled off as soon as the door to the building shut. I parked across the street, so I could see everything that was going on.

***

Porsche

I sat behind the dark tints of the van, watching as Dr. Ross fiddled with his keys to unlock the front door. I had parked the van backwards in the parking space. I watched as Money's mother climbed out the truck with a smile on her face as she scrolled inside the office.

After waiting five minutes, I exited the van and played with the locks and walked inside. I took out my Glock 17 and crept along the wall to the back where I cracked open the door to the office. Money's mother was bent over, taking the dick from the back. I wasn't a hater. I just watched.

Baby, this is the best pussy a man can ask for," Dr. Ross said, pumping.

"I'm cumming," Money's mother moaned.

"Me too."

"Glad y'all got that out of the way," I said.

Dr. Ross jumped up, surprised to see someone else in his office besides them two.

"Who are you, and what you want?" he asked, covering his dick.

"To be old, you is carrying better than some young niggas I know," I said, walking all the way inside.

"I said who are you, and what you want?" Dr. Ross yelled.

"Since you want to yell, I got something for you. Put your hand up," I told Dr. Ross.

He did as he was told and just like that, two bullets in the nuts.

"You, let's get out of here," I told Money's mother at gunpoint. She never put up a fight as she walked to the back of the van.

As soon as the back doors opened, I slapped her in the back of her head, knocking her out cold. I then began to tie and tape her up. Hopping in, I rushed to get to our meeting spot. On my way, I phoned Queen and SK.

"Hello?" Queen picked up.

"My end is complete, and I'm on my way to the meeting spot, so hurry up and get y'all shit done. He should be pulling up by now," I said.

***

Queen

I knew Lil' Nate and Sade were in their positions, waiting on the right moment to move. He was in the bathroom, watching the main door. I sent him a text saying showtime.

The Feds bent the corner slowly and stopped at the curb. I sat there, watching Money get out and help the boys down one by one. They walked inside the building just as SK parked the UPS truck.

***

SK

When I walked inside the school, all I saw was kids everywhere. I entered the main office just in time to see Money sign the boys in. A few minutes later, Karen walked into the office.

"Hello, boys." Karen spoke to them.

"Hey." They both spoke back.

Money bent down to give both boys hugs and a kiss before sending them on their way.

"Y'all be good today," he yelled.

They just smiled and waved their hands.

***

Karen

When they turned the corner, I rushed the boys down the stairwell where Sade was waiting on me. After I handed the boys over, Sade took control of them. She made it to the door in no time.

I watched Queen smile at the sight of Sade coming out the door.

***

SK

"Aye, my man, check this out for a hot second," I said, holding my phone up and out for Money to see.

It was a video that Porsche had just sent me. There was a note taped to his mother's chest that said, "Ya better not tip anyone." Money looked at the phone again then back at me. The phone began to ring.

"Go head and talk," I said.

"Hello?" Money's voice shook.

"What's up, bitch ass nigga?" Queen asked.

"Queen. What's… What's goin' on?" he asked.

"Look, nigga, you always playing crazy, like you don't know what's going on. Well, I have your mother and boys, so if you want them alive, you need to do whatever the nice man tell you to do," she said.

Money followed me out of the office and to a waiting Lil' Nate.

"Follow him," I said, pointing to Lil' Nate.

***

Lil' Nate

I grabbed Money's arm and pulled him down the hall, not caring. I shoved Money all the way to the car where I knocked him out with a two piece to the jaw.

Chapter 29

Queen

"Wake your ass up," SK said, throwing a bowl full of cold water on Money.

"What's going on?" Money asked, coming out of his knockout.

"Nigga, you in hell. You're a rat ass nigga. You have every police in this city looking for me and my people," I said.

Money's eyes began to see clearly, and he saw that his mother was tied to a chair also.

"No, not my mother. Her and my boys have nothing to do with this," Money said.

"No, no, no. They have everything to do with it. Not only did she give birth to your bitch ass, but she been right by your side the whole time you been ratting on us," I said, bending down to look into his eyes.

"You know what, Money? Queen saved you too many times, but now, you have me into all this bullshit too, so she can't save that ass this time. You have me out here running for my life because you can't hold shit in the streets like a thug. I should blow your mother's head off, but I'm going to wait on that," Porsche said.

"Queen, I know I fucked up, and I know you plan to kill us, but I want you to know that if you kill the boys, you will be killing your cousin and brother," Money said.

"What the fuck you just say?" I asked.

"So, Kenya never told you about your little brother?" Money asked, laughing.

I slapped fire from Money's mouth.

"Omar is your brother. That's why he's named after y'all daddy. When you went away to prison, Big Jesus is the one that got your mother hooked on the drugs, then she became his sex toy. When she couldn't pay for the drugs, he made her work for it," Money said.

"This nigga is lying. He's saying anything to save himself from getting killed," Porsche said, pacing the floor.

"No, I'm not lying. Call your mother and ask her about it," he said to me.

I grabbed my phone and went into the same room the little boy was sleeping in and hit the FaceTime for Kenya. When her face popped on the screen, I went in.

"Mommy, let me know the truth. I don't want any sugarcoating nothing either," I said, crying.

"Queen, what you talking about?" she asked.

"Is this my little brother?" I asked, putting the sleeping boy on the screen.

I could tell by the way her face moved that it was true.

"How could you disrespect me, my father, and yourself by doing this shit?" I screamed.

"Calm down, Queen, let me explain. I was down bad, and yes, I was on dope fiend shit, and when I couldn't pay for it, I slept for it. Big Jesus kept on pushing dope in my hands, but when I got knocked up, I hid from everyone, but then, Big Jesus found out. He took the baby as soon as I pushed him out of my pussy. He gave the baby to Marilyn and Money to raise as their own. I didn't care because he wasn't from your father, so please forgive me," Kenya said, crying.

"But why give him my daddy's name?" I asked.

"I don't know, baby."

I was so hurt over this, but I knew how it was on drugs.

"We will talk later," I said, hanging up.

"It's all true," I said, walking into the room.

"I told you so," Money said.

"So, what now?" asked Porsche.

"We make this nigga talk," I said.

Porsche stood over Money's mother with her Glock 17 pointed at her head.

"Now, what have you told them police?" I asked.

"Nothing really," he said.

"Keep lying and Porsche goin' to kill you."

"I said nothing."

"Pow. Pow."

To Be Continued in Part 3

Lock Down Publications and Ca$h Presents
Assisted Publishing Packages

Due to an increase in the price of services we have increased our prices. The prices below reflect the price increase as of 11/1/24.

BASIC PACKAGE	UPGRADED PACKAGE
$699	**$1000**
Editing	Typing
Cover Design	Editing
Formatting	Cover Design
	Formatting
	Upload eBooks to Amazon
	Upload Paperback to Amazon
ADVANCE PACKAGE	**LDP SUPREME PACKAGE**
$1,400	**$1,700**
Typing	Typing
Editing (line editing/content)	Editing (line editing/content)
Cover Design	Cover Design
Formatting	Formatting
Copyright Registration	Copyright Registration
Proofreading	Proofreading
Upload eBooks to Amazon	Set up Amazon Account
Upload Paperback to Amazon	Upload eBooks to Amazon
	Upload Paperback to Amazon
	Advertise on LDP's Amazon and Facebook Page

***

Other services available upon request.
Additional charges may apply

Lock Down Publications
P.O. Box 944
Stockbridge, GA 30281-9998
Phone: 470 303-9761
Email: lockdownpublications@gmail.com

Submission Guideline

Submit the first three chapters of your completed manuscript to ldpsubmissions@gmail.com. In the subject line add **Your Book's Title**. The manuscript must be in a Word Doc file and sent as an attachment. Document should be in Times New Roman, double spaced, and in size 12 font. Also, provide your synopsis and full contact information. If sending multiple submissions, they must each be in a separate email.

Have a story but no way to send it electronically? You can still submit to LDP/Ca$h Presents. Send in the first three chapters, written or typed, of your completed manuscript to:

LDP: Submissions Dept
P.O. Box 944
Stockbridge, GA 30281-9998

DO NOT send original manuscript. Must be a duplicate. Provide your synopsis and a cover letter containing your full contact information.

Thanks for considering LDP and Ca$h Presents.

NEW RELEASES

BLOODLINE OF A SAVAGE 1-3
THESE VICIOUS STREETS 1-3
RELENTLESS GOON 1-3
BY PRINCE A. TAUHID

THE BUTTERFLY MAFIA 1-3
BY FUMIYA PAYNE

A THUG'S STREET PRINCESS 1&2
BY MEESHA

CITY OF SMOKE 3
BY MOLOTTI

GET IT IN SLUGS 1 &2
BY B. STALL

STANDING ON HER BUSINESS 1&2
BY DG SANTANA

STEPPERS 1,2&3
THE REAL BADDIES OF CHI-RAQ
BY KING RIO

THE LANE 1&2
BY KEN-KEN SPENCE

THUG OF SPADES 1&2
LOVE IN THE TRENCHES 2
CORNER BOYS
BY COREY ROBINSON

TIL DEATH 3
BY ARYANNA

QUEEN OF NAPTOWN 2 | KEITH CHANDLER

THE BIRTH OF A GANGSTER 4
BY DELMONT PLAYER

PRODUCT OF THE STREETS 1-3
BY DEMOND "MONEY" ANDERSON

NO TIME FOR ERROR
BY KEESE

MONEY HUNGRY DEMONS 1-2
BY TRANAY ADAMS

HUB CITY MENACE 1-3
BY J. WHITE

A THUGGISH PASSION 1&2
LAND OF DA HOOLIGANZ 1-4
KILLAZ ON STANDBY 1&2
BY IRA B.

FO'EVA ROLLIN 1&2
BY ASSA RAYMOND BAKER

THE LEVEL UP 1&3
BY LUXURY KING

Coming Soon from Lock Down Publications/Ca$h Presents

IF YOU CROSS ME ONCE 6
ANGEL V
By Anthony Fields

A THUGS STREET PRINCESS 3
By Meesha

CORNER BOYS 2
By Corey Robinson

THA TAKEOVER
By Keith Chandler

BETRAYAL OF A G 2
By Ray Vinci

SAVAGE FAMILY EMPIRE 1&2
SOULLESS GOON 1,2&3
THE DIRTY SIDE OF MONEY 1,2&3
By Prince

FOR MY ENEMY'S SAKE
AMBITIONS OF A SLIDER
FRESH OFF DA PORCH
By IRA B.

THE TRUCKLOAD 1-4
TIPPIN' THE SCALES 1-3
BAD BITCHES WIT GUNZ 3
PROBLEM SOLVED 2
By Christopher "Diesel" Hornezes

Available Now

RESTRAINING ORDER 1 & 2
By **CA$H & Coffee**

LOVE KNOWS NO BOUNDARIES 1-3
By **Coffee**

RAISED AS A GOON I, II, III & IV
BRED BY THE SLUMS I, II, III
BLAST FOR ME I & II
ROTTEN TO THE CORE I II III
A BRONX TALE I, II, III
DUFFLE BAG CARTEL I II III IV V VI
HEARTLESS GOON I II III IV V
A SAVAGE DOPEBOY I II
DRUG LORDS I II III
CUTTHROAT MAFIA I II
KING OF THE TRENCHES
By **Ghost**

LAY IT DOWN I & II
LAST OF A DYING BREED I II
BLOOD STAINS OF A SHOTTA I & II III
By **Jamaica**

LOYAL TO THE GAME I II III
LIFE OF SIN I, II III
By **TJ & Jelissa**

IF LOVING HIM IS WRONG...I & II
LOVE ME EVEN WHEN IT HURTS I II III
By **Jelissa**

PUSH IT TO THE LIMIT
By **Bre' Hayes**

BLOODY COMMAS I & II
SKI MASK CARTEL I, II & III
KING OF NEW YORK I II, III IV V
RISE TO POWER I II III
COKE KINGS I II III IV V
BORN HEARTLESS I II III IV
KING OF THE TRAP I II
By **T.J. Edwards**

WHEN THE STREETS CLAP BACK I & II III
THE HEART OF A SAVAGE I II III IV
MONEY MAFIA I II
LOYAL TO THE SOIL I II III
By **Jibril Williams**

A DISTINGUISHED THUG STOLE MY HEART I II & III
LOVE SHOULDN'T HURT I II III IV
RENEGADE BOYS 1-4
PAID IN KARMA 1-3
SAVAGE STORMS 1-3
AN UNFORESEEN LOVE 1-3
BABY, I'M WINTERTIME COLD 1-3
A THUG'S STREET PRINCESS 1&2
By **Meesha**

A GANGSTER'S CODE 1-3
A GANGSTER'S SYN 1-3
THE SAVAGE LIFE 1-3
CHAINED TO THE STREETS 1-3
BLOOD ON THE MONEY 1-3
A GANGSTA'S PAIN 1-3
BEAUTIFUL LIES AND UGLY TRUTHS
CHURCH IN THESE STREETS
By **J-Blunt**

CUM FOR ME 1-8
An LDP Erotica Collaboration

BLOOD OF A BOSS 1-5
SHADOWS OF THE GAME
TRAP BASTARD
By **Askari**

THE STREETS BLEED MURDER 1-3
THE HEART OF A GANGSTA 1-3
By **Jerry Jackson**

WHEN A GOOD GIRL GOES BAD
By **Adrienne**

THE COST OF LOYALTY 1-3
By **Kweli**

BRIDE OF A HUSTLA 1-3
THE FETTI GIRLS 1-3
CORRUPTED BY A GANGSTA 1-4
BLINDED BY HIS LOVE
THE PRICE YOU PAY FOR LOVE 1-3
DOPE GIRL MAGIC 1-3
By **Destiny Skai**

A KINGPIN'S AMBITION
A KINGPIN'S AMBITION II
I MURDER FOR THE DOUGH
By **Ambitious**

TRUE SAVAGE 1-7
DOPE BOY MAGIC 1-3
MIDNIGHT CARTEL 1-3
CITY OF KINGZ 1&2
NIGHTMARE ON SILENT AVE
THE PLUG OF LIL MEXICO 1&2
CLASSIC CITY
By **Chris Green**

A GANGSTER'S REVENGE 1-4
THE BOSS MAN'S DAUGHTERS 1-5
A SAVAGE LOVE 1&2
BAE BELONGS TO ME 1&2
A HUSTLER'S DECEIT 1-3
WHAT BAD BITCHES DO 1-3
SOUL OF A MONSTER 1-3
KILL ZONE
A DOPE BOY'S QUEEN 1-3
TIL DEATH 1-3
IMMA DIE BOUT MINE 1-6
DYING FOR LIKES
By **Aryanna**

A DOPEBOY'S PRAYER
By **Eddie "Wolf" Lee**

THE KING CARTEL 1-3
By **Frank Gresham**

THESE NIGGAS AIN'T LOYAL 1-3
By **Nikki Tee**

GANGSTA SHYT 1-3
By **CATO**

THE ULTIMATE BETRAYAL
By **Phoenix**

BOSS'N UP 1-3
By **Royal Nicole**

I LOVE YOU TO DEATH
By **Destiny J**

I RIDE FOR MY HITTA
I STILL RIDE FOR MY HITTA
By **Misty Holt**

LOVE & CHASIN' PAPER
By **Qay Crockett**

TO DIE IN VAIN
SINS OF A HUSTLA
By **ASAD**

BROOKLYN HUSTLAZ
By **Boogsy Morina**

BROOKLYN ON LOCK 1 & 2
By **Sonovia**

GANGSTA CITY
By **Teddy Duke**

A DRUG KING AND HIS DIAMOND 1-3
A DOPEMAN'S RICHES
HER MAN, MINE'S TOO 1&2
CASH MONEY HO'S
THE WIFEY I USED TO BE 1&2
PRETTY GIRLS DO NASTY THINGS
By **Nicole Goosby**

LIPSTICK KILLAH 1-3
CRIME OF PASSION 1-3
FRIEND OR FOE 1-3
By **Mimi**

TRAPHOUSE KING 1-3
KINGPIN KILLAZ 1-3
STREET KINGS 1&2
PAID IN BLOOD 1&2
CARTEL KILLAZ 1-3
DOPE GODS 1&2
By **Hood Rich**

THE STREETS ARE CALLING
By **Duquie Wilson**

STEADY MOBBN' 1-3
THE STREETS STAINED MY SOUL 1-3
By **Marcellus Allen**

WHO SHOT YA 1-3
SON OF A DOPE FIEND 1-4
HEAVEN GOT A GHETTO 1&2
SKI MASK MONEY 1&2
By **Renta**

GORILLAZ IN THE BAY 1-4
TEARS OF A GANGSTA 1/&2
3X KRAZY 1&2
STRAIGHT BEAST MODE 1&2
By **DE'KARI**

TRIGGADALE 1-3
MURDA WAS THE CASE 1-3
By **Elijah R. Freeman**

SLAUGHTER GANG 1-3
RUTHLESS HEART 1-3
By **Willie Slaughter**

GOD BLESS THE TRAPPERS 1-3
THESE SCANDALOUS STREETS 1-3
FEAR MY GANGSTA 1-5
THESE STREETS DON'T LOVE NOBODY 1-2
BURY ME A G 1-5
A GANGSTA'S EMPIRE 1-4
THE DOPEMAN'S BODYGAURD 1&2
THE REALEST KILLAZ 1-3
THE LAST OF THE OGS 1-3
By **Tranay Adams**

MARRIED TO A BOSS 1-3
By **Destiny Skai & Chris Green**

KINGZ OF THE GAME 1-7
CRIME BOSS 1-4
By **Playa Ray**

FUK SHYT
By **Blakk Diamond**

DON'T F#CK WITH MY HEART 1&2
By **Linnea**

ADDICTED TO THE DRAMA 1-3
IN THE ARM OF HIS BOSS
By **Jamila**

LOYALTY AIN'T PROMISED 1&2
By **Keith Williams**

YAYO 1-4
A SHOOTER'S AMBITION 1&2
BRED IN THE GAME
By **S. Allen**

TRAP GOD 1-3
RICH $AVAGE 1-3
MONEY IN THE GRAVE 1-3
CARTEL MONEY 1&2
By **Martell Troublesome Bolden**

FOREVER GANGSTA 1&2
GLOCKS ON SATIN SHEETS 1&2
By **Adrian Dulan**

TOE TAGZ 1-4
LEVELS TO THIS SHYT 1&2
IT'S JUST ME AND YOU
By **Ah'Million**

KINGPIN DREAMS 1-3
RAN OFF ON DA PLUG
By **Paper Boi Rari**

THE STREETS MADE ME 1-3
By **Larry D. Wright**

CONFESSIONS OF A GANGSTA 1-4
CONFESSIONS OF A JACKBOY 1-3
CONFESSIONS OF A HITMAN
CONFESSIONS OF A DOPE BOY
By **Nicholas Lock**

I'M NOTHING WITHOUT HIS LOVE
SINS OF A THUG
TO THE THUG I LOVED BEFORE
A GANGSTA SAVED XMAS
IN A HUSTLER I TRUST
By **Monet Dragun**

QUIET MONEY 1-3
THUG LIFE 1-3
EXTENDED CLIP 1&2
A GANGSTA'S PARADISE
By **Trai'Quan**

CAUGHT UP IN THE LIFE 1-3
THE STREETS NEVER LET GO 1-3
By **Robert Baptiste**

NEW TO THE GAME 1-3
MONEY, MURDER & MEMORIES 1-3
By **Malik D. Rice**

CREAM 2-3
THE STREETS WILL TALK
By **Yolanda Moore**

THE STREETS WILL NEVER CLOSE 1-3
By **K'ajji**

LIFE OF A SAVAGE 1-4
A GANGSTA'S QUR'AN 1-4
MURDA SEASON 1-3
GANGLAND CARTEL 1-3
CHI'RAQ GANGSTAS 1-4
KILLERS ON ELM STREET 1-3
JACK BOYZ N DA BRONX 1-3
A DOPEBOY'S DREAM 1-3
JACK BOYS VS DOPE BOYS 1-3
COKE GIRLZ
COKE BOYS
SOSA GANG 1&2
BRONX SAVAGES
BODYMORE KINGPINS
BLOOD OF A GOON
By **Romell Tukes**

CONCRETE KILLA 1-3
VICIOUS LOYALTY 1-3
BLOODY MONEY BAGS
By **Kingpen**

THE ULTIMATE SACRIFICE 1-6
KHADIFI
IF YOU CROSS ME ONCE 1-3
ANGEL 1-4
IN THE BLINK OF AN EYE
By **Anthony Fields**

THE LIFE OF A HOOD STAR
By **Ca$h & Rashia Wilson**

NIGHTMARES OF A HUSTLA 1-3
BLOOD AND GAMES 1&2
By **King Dream**

GHOST MOB
By **Stilloan Robinson**

HARD AND RUTHLESS 1&2
MOB TOWN 251
THE BILLIONAIRE BENTLEYS 1-3
REAL G'S MOVE IN SILENCE
By **Von Diesel**

MOB TIES 1-7
SOUL OF A HUSTLER, HEART OF A KILLER 1-3
GORILLAZ IN THE TRENCHES
OOPS CRY TOO 1&2
THE DAUGHTER OF A CARTEL BOSS
By **SayNoMore**

BODYMORE MURDERLAND 1-3
THE BIRTH OF A GANGSTER 1-4
By **Delmont Player**

FOR THE LOVE OF A BOSS 1&2
By **C. D. Blue**

KILLA KOUNTY 1-5
TENDER
By **Khufu**

MOBBED UP 1-4
THE BRICK MAN 1-5
THE COCAINE PRINCESS 1-10
STEPPERS 1-3
SUPER GREMLIN 1-4
A GANGSTA'S SON
By **King Rio**

MONEY GAME 1&2
By **Smoove Dolla**

A GANGSTA'S KARMA 1-5
By **FLAME**

KING OF THE TRENCHES 1-3
By **GHOST & TRANAY ADAMS**

BAD BITCHES WIT GUNZ 1&2
PROBLEM SOLVED
By "Christopher Diesel" Hornezes

QUEEN OF THE ZOO 1&2
By **Black Migo**

GRIMEY WAYS 1-3
BETRAYAL OF A G
By **Ray Vinci**

XMAS WITH AN ATL SHOOTER
By **Ca$h & Destiny Skai**

KING KILLA 1&2
By **Vincent "Vitto" Holloway**

BETRAYAL OF A THUG 1&2
By **Fre$h**

COUNTDOWN OF A KILLA 1&2
SEX, MURDER AND GOD 1&2
GUNS DOWN, BOTTOMS UP 1&2
By Lo-Life

THE MURDER QUEENS 1-7
By **Michael Gallon**

FOR THE LOVE OF BLOOD 1-4
By **Jamel Mitchell**

HOOD CONSIGLIERE 1&2
NO TIME FOR ERROR
By **Keese**

PROTÉGÉ OF A LEGEND 1,2&3
LOVE IN THE TRENCHES 1&2
By **Corey Robinson**

THE PLUG'S RUTHLESS DAUGHTER 1&2
By **Tony Daniels**

BORN IN THE GRAVE 1-3
CRIME PAYS
By **Self Made Tay**

MOAN IN MY MOUTH
By **XTASY**

TORN BETWEEN A GANGSTER AND A GENTLEMAN
By **J-BLUNT & Miss Kim**

LOYALTY IS EVERYTHING 1-3
CITY OF SMOKE 1-3
By **Molotti**

HERE TODAY GONE TOMORROW 1&2
By **Fly Rock**

WOMEN LIE MEN LIE 1-4
FIFTY SHADES OF SNOW 1-3
STACK BEFORE YOU SPLURGE
GIRLS FALL LIKE DOMINOES
NAÏVE TO THE STREETS
By **ROY MILLIGAN**

PILLOW PRINCESS
By **S. Hawkins**

THE BUTTERFLY MAFIA 1-3
SALUTE MY SAVAGERY 1&2
By **Fumiya Payne**

THE LANE 1&2
By Ken-Ken Spence

THE PUSSY TRAP 1-5
By **Nene Capri**

DIRTY DNA
By **Blaque**

SANCTIFIED AND HORNY
by **XTASY**

BOOKS BY LDP'S CEO, CA$H

TRUST IN NO MAN
TRUST IN NO MAN 2
TRUST IN NO MAN 3
BONDED BY BLOOD
SHORTY GOT A THUG
THUGS CRY
THUGS CRY 2
THUGS CRY 3
TRUST NO BITCH
TRUST NO BITCH 2
TRUST NO BITCH 3
TIL MY CASKET DROPS
RESTRAINING ORDER
RESTRAINING ORDER 2
IN LOVE WITH A CONVICT
LIFE OF A HOOD STAR
XMAS WITH AN ATL SHOOTER

www.ingramcontent.com/pod-product-compliance
Lightning Source LLC
Chambersburg PA
CBHW071225260626
47162CB00004B/1431